Major Bricket
and the Circus Corpse

Also by Simon Brett

Blotto, Twinks and the Ex-King's Daughter

Blotto, Twinks and the Dead Dowager Duchess

Blotto, Twinks and the Rodents of the Riviera

Blotto, Twinks and the Bootlegger's Moll

Blotto, Twinks and the Riddle of the Sphinx

Blotto, Twinks and the Heir to the Tsar

Blotto, Twinks and the Stars of the Silver Screen

Blotto, Twinks and the Intimate Revue

Blotto, Twinks and the Great Road Race

Blotto, Twinks and the Maharajah's Jewel

Blotto, Twinks and the Suspicious Guests

Blotto, Twinks and the Conquistadors' Gold

Blotto, Twinks and the Phantom Skiers

Major Bricket
and the Circus Corpse

SIMON BRETT

CONSTABLE

First published in Great Britain in 2025 by Constable

3 5 7 9 10 8 6 4 2

Copyright © Simon Brett, 2025

The moral right of the author has been asserted.

*All characters and events in this publication, other than
those clearly in the public domain, are fictitious
and any resemblance to real persons,
living or dead, is purely coincidental.*

All rights reserved.
No part of this publication may be reproduced, stored in a retrieval system, or transmitted, in any form, or by any means, without the prior permission in writing of the publisher, nor be otherwise circulated in any form of binding or cover other than that in which it is published and without a similar condition including this condition being imposed on the subsequent purchaser.

A CIP catalogue record for this book
is available from the British Library.

ISBN: 978-1-40872-130-8

Typeset by Initial Typesetting Services, Edinburgh
Printed and bound in Great Britain by Clays Ltd, Elcograf S.p.A.

Papers used by Constable are from well-managed forests
and other responsible sources.

Constable
An imprint of
Little, Brown Book Group
Carmelite House
50 Victoria Embankment
London EC4Y 0DZ

The authorised representative
in the EEA is
Hachette Ireland
8 Castlecourt Centre, Dublin 15,
D15 XTP3, Ireland
(email: info@hbgi.ie)

An Hachette UK Company
www.hachette.co.uk

www.littlebrown.co.uk

*To Lisa,
who had faith in the idea,
with love*

1

The Traveller Returns

'The job is a simple murder,' said the Employer.

'Very well,' said the Employee.

'Do you know the village of Stunston Peveril?'

'Not well, but I have been there.'

'Good. The instructions will be sent as a voice message to your mobile phone.'

'Are there any unusual demands as to how the murder is done?'

'You will see that when you receive the voice message.'

'Very well,' said the Employee. 'And when do you want it done?'

'That too will be in the voice message,' said the Employer. 'As soon as you receive it, I want you to memorise the contents and then delete the message.'

'Very well. So, it's just your standard village murder, is it?' asked the Employee.

'Oh, it's rather different from that,' said the Employer.

'Major Bricket's going to be living in Stunston Peveril all the time,' Venetia Clothbury announced definitively.

'Oh, where did you hear that?' asked her friend Mollie Greenford.

'I have my sources,' came the mysterious reply.

Mollie nodded sagely. She had long since learnt that, if you wanted to stay a friend of Venetia Clothbury, it was unwise to disagree with her. And, even though she wouldn't exactly have said that she *liked* Venetia, she did want to stay her friend. There wasn't a huge choice of friends in a Suffolk village like Stunston Peveril. And the older ones did have an inconvenient habit of dying off. Most, though not all, from natural causes.

The two octogenarians were having their regular Monday morning coffee at the Gingham Tea Shop. Stunston Peveril was too small to have been colonised by one of the global coffee chains like Starbucks, and for over twenty years the Gingham Tea Shop had supplied its needs in hot beverages, fancy cakes and fanciful gossip. It was run with beady efficiency by Elvira Finchcombe, who was always hinting she came from a titled family and who discouraged the invasion of her premises by tourists with sleeveless Union Jack T-shirts and tattoos.

'It's interesting that Major Bricket is coming back. It must mean that he's retired.' Venetia Clothbury always spoke at full volume. This was not because she was deaf – nor indeed because Mollie Greenford was deaf. It was simply that it never occurred to Venetia that other people might not be interested in what she had to say.

This had certainly been the case with her deceased husband, Sydney, an Old Etonian whose pinched face had always exhibited the discomfort of a man whose entire married life had been spent trying – unsuccessfully – to get a word in edgeways.

'Retired from what, though?' asked Mollie. 'Nobody in the village seems to know what he actually did.'

'Oh, I do,' Venetia Clothbury asserted.

'How clever of you to find out,' said Mollie.

'Yes, it was,' her friend agreed.

'I've heard a lot of theories from people in the village,' said Mollie. 'Some say he's involved in import/export.'

'"Import/export" of what?'

'Oh, they didn't say that. Other people say he works for Interpol.'

'Doing what?'

'Oh, they didn't say that. And then Rhona in Cosy Collectibles says Major Bricket arranges the touring schedules for an international orchestra. That's why he's away so much.'

'Nonsense.'

'And Lena who cleans at the vicarage says the Major's a television producer. He does those programmes where celebrities are shut away in the jungle and made to eat insects.'

Venetia Clothbury shuddered. 'How irredeemably vulgar.'

'I agree,' said Mollie. 'Programmes like that are an insult to my intelligence.'

'Imagine what they do to mine,' said her friend loftily.

'And then Dierdre in the Post Office says the Major writes romance novels under a female pen name and he travels to research them.'

'Well, as it happens, Mollie, they're all wrong,' Venetia Clothbury pronounced with her customary unassailable self-belief. 'Major Bricket is in fact in the direct employ of Buckingham Palace. His travels are all to check on the security before Royal visits.'

'Oh,' said Mollie Greenford admiringly. 'You know everything.'

Venetia Clothbury smiled smugly. She had never been a woman to let ignorance of the subject matter get in the way of her pronouncements.

'No trouble down at Ratchetts Common yet?' asked Gregory, Viscount Wintle, gloomily.

He was sitting in the Yellow Morning Room of Fincham Abbey, a space whose patina of dust and draping of cobwebs bore witness to the fact that the Wintles had insufficient staff. The Viscount was looking out of the windows over his estate, now considerably reduced from the hundreds of acres owned by earlier generations of the family. Many parcels of land had been sold off to pay death duties, particularly in the years after the Second World War. Though the view from the Yellow Morning Room was unspoilt, the Viscount was never unaware of the housing estates encroaching on either side of the diminished gardens he had left. Those housing estates, it should be said, made a great deal more profit for their developers than the sale of the land ever had for the Wintle family.

'There won't be any trouble,' said his wife, Perpetua. Her voice was soothing, a tone she adopted for most conversations with her husband. The Viscount lived in constant anticipation of new disasters. His view was that, during the seventy-odd years of his lifetime, Great Britain had 'gone to hell in a handcart'. He'd had no respect for any politician since Margaret Thatcher and regarded all governments since then as conspiracies against the upper classes. He entertained a sneaking nostalgia for the feudal system, when at least everyone knew their place.

He was dressed that morning in his uniform of a tweed suit, which had been distressed even back when his father wore it. The collar of his Tattersall shirt was frayed, and the white lining showed through the silk at the edges of his regimental tie. The leather of his brogues was cracked but still highly polished.

The state of Gregory's attire had nothing to do with poverty. Though he was constantly complaining about not having enough money, he was of the class that made a fetish of dressing scruffily. Clothes, like furniture, should, in his view, be inherited.

Perpetua, by way of contrast, had on a summer dress, whose white background was decorated with a design of forget-me-nots. She wore thick stockings and shoes suitable for dog-walking. Grey hair was swept back in what used to be called an Alice band. Her face was innocent of make-up but its leathery surface bore witness to a life spent mostly outdoors. The couple's two children had long since left home. Son Henry made money in the City, and daughter Serena was currently occupied with her small children and would be until they were old enough to join the Pony Club.

The Viscount and Viscountess had got beyond the point in their marriage when they might notice each other's appearance. And both were so short-sighted that to each of them the other was only a blurred outline, anyway. Both still drove battered Land Rovers along the lanes of Suffolk, ever-present hazards to all other road-users.

If either Wintle had been asked the rather impertinent question, both the Viscount and Viscountess would have asserted that they had a very happy marriage. But this did not prevent Gregory constantly moaning at Perpetua.

After more than forty years, she had heard all his moans many times before.

There were the continuing ones. Any time of year he could be heard moaning that they couldn't afford the proper number of staff for a place like Fincham Abbey. They hadn't even got a butler, for God's sake.

And then there were the moans that came round on an annual cycle. Perpetua could predict, almost to the hour, that, come July, their subject would be Ratchetts Common.

Despite the implication of its name, Ratchetts Common was not in public ownership, but part of the Fincham Abbey estate. An open area abutting the village of Stunston Peveril, it had never been cultivated, though in more leisured times it had given space to tennis courts and croquet lawns. And every July, it played host to the Stunston Peveril Summer Fair. Which, every July, Gregory complained about.

The summer fair was a surprisingly lavish event for such a diminutive village. As well as a few stalls manned by locals, it featured a small travelling circus, with a ring master and such old-fashioned acts as clowns, trapeze artistes, a strongman and a knife-thrower. The ownership of Lavoisier's Circus had gone through many generations of the family, until it came to the current incumbent, Bernard Lavoisier. Rumour had it that he was more interested in the booze than the family business. Certainly, while he was in the village, he spent a lot of time at its only pub. Each morning, he left his caravan on Ratchetts Common and was inside the Goat & Compasses the minute it opened.

Along with the circus, there was also a funfair, featuring

a range of old-fashioned stalls: coconut shies, whack-a-moles – even a mini-helter-skelter and dodgems. The summer fair was a fixture in the calendar, attracting visitors from many of the nearby towns in that part of Suffolk. The seven days it was encamped in Stunston Peveril contributed healthily to the local economy.

And its popularity seemed to grow rather than diminish. Wealthy people with second homes in East Anglia were attracted to such old-fashioned entertainments as a kind of retro chic. It exerted a similar pull to Cromer's End-of-the-Pier Variety Show.

On Perpetua's initiative, soon after she married Gregory, the summer fair had been invited to use Ratchetts Common. Their previous site, an empty area behind the church, had been bought for development. So, without Perpetua's intervention, Stunston Peveril would have lost its summer fair. And, though its presence did not affect the even tenor of his life one iota, Gregory felt it a point of honour to complain every year about 'having all that riffraff on Ratchetts Common'.

Every year, his wife listened to the moans with her customary apparent interest, tact and steely determination to get her own way. She had no worries that, with regard to the summer fair, she might have to make any changes to the *status quo*. Perpetua Wintle had decided, even before their marriage, that, at Fincham Abbey, she would be the one who wore the threadbare corduroy trousers.

The summer fair coincided with a social event about which Gregory felt a lot happier. Indeed, he welcomed it. The Fincham Abbey Costume Ball was a tradition in the Wintle family, dating back to the Roaring Twenties. Except for an unavoidable break during the Second

World War, the event had taken place every year since. For historical reasons, which no one could now remember, it had always taken place on a Monday. Gregory had made his first appearance, dressed as a page boy, at the age of four. And, though he felt a duty to complain every year about the disruption caused by the costume ball, it was actually one of the highlights of his social calendar. He derived childlike glee from coming up with ever more bizarre costumes for himself.

The other attraction of the event for him was that the guest list only included 'his kind of people'. Though Viscount Wintle would hotly deny the accusation, had it ever been raised, he was in fact a terrible snob. His wife was constantly building bridges with the people of Stunston Peveril, but her husband's unspoken desire was to blow all of those bridges up. He could be polite to the locals at events like the opening of the summer fair, but he never felt that they were members of his tribe. He was always more at ease with the Etonians and Harrovians he had grown up with.

And so, it was their names that filled the costume ball's guest list. Of the Stunston Peveril locals, only a tiny handful were thought worthy of receiving a stiff invitation card through their letterboxes. And they were instantly dropped off the list if they were ever heard to refer to the event as 'fancy dress'. Viscount Wintle had his standards.

For him, another great attraction of the Fincham Abbey Costume Ball was that his only input to the preparations was deciding what to wear. Not that this was a minor task for the Viscount. It was something he puzzled over for much of the year between balls. Normally, he homed in quite early in the process on the character he would represent. But finding the perfect costume for that character could be a long undertaking. He had been known to order up to a dozen variations from different theatrical costumiers, and only decide which one to wear on the evening of the ball.

He still hadn't made the vital decision for the current one. But that was all he had to worry about. As in so many areas of their lives, Perpetua had made all the other arrangements for this massive annual jamboree.

Gregory Wintle was entirely happy about his wife organising everything, with a few significant exceptions. He had always drawn a strict line between what he regarded as 'men's work' and what he regarded as 'women's work'. And he was untroubled by the way, gradually during the years of their marriage, an increasing number of responsibilities had been shifted from the first category to the second.

Some duties he still guarded as his own, though. The sporting facilities for weekend guests, of whom there were fewer and fewer over time, the Viscount regarded as exclusively his province. If setting up a shooting party or fishing expedition, he knew the right people, gamekeepers and such, to whom to delegate the actual arrangements.

Gregory Wintle also claimed he was responsible for anything to do with the fabric of the building. Fincham Abbey had been in his family for so long that he felt it to be almost a part of his body, so when structural work was required, he it was who would consult builders and get estimates, generally far in excess of anything the family could afford. Letting the great building quietly collapse into disrepair was, undoubtedly in the Viscount's estimation, 'men's work'. As was paying the regular bills that were inescapable with a property of that size and age. Necessary minor repairs, windows being cleaned less often than they should be, insurance, burglar alarms being checked... all such expenses were paid by Gregory. And, long after most of the world had moved on to online banking, Viscount Wintle made a point of paying by cheque. His cheques were written in fountain pen and posted to their destinations in envelopes. With stamps on them.

Perpetua did, on occasion, question her husband about whether he was keeping up to date with all the bills. Though she would never put the criticism into words, she didn't have complete confidence in Gregory's reliability in matters of detail.

Such enquiries, however, only served to engender considerable anger in her husband, so, in the cause of domestic harmony, she stopped making them. And crossed her fingers, in the hope that all the regular demands were being met.

She also very soon backed off making suggestions that their financial situation might be eased by selling off some of Fincham Abbey's works of art. The walls were decked with dusty, ill-lit family portraits and other paintings, some of which knowledgeable weekend guests had identified as treasures. They had not been catalogued or valued for many decades, but the Viscount would not tolerate any talk of selling even the smallest of them. Like the building itself, they were an essential component of his identity. So, as she had many times in their marriage, the Viscountess once again bit her tongue.

Perpetua's expertise in the running of Fincham Abbey

was part of the way she had been bred. She'd inherited that upper-class skill of making very complex tasks look effortless. Which meant that, on the morning of the ball, while staff shifted furniture in the abbey's Great Hall, brought up bottles of vintage champagne from the abbey's wine cellars and prepared delicious food in the abbey's kitchens, she could take time to sit in the Yellow Morning Room listening to her husband moan about the summer fair.

Gregory was never one to give up after a single moan. He picked further at the old scab by saying, 'Well, one day there will be trouble down at Ratchetts Common, you mark my word. You can't invite a criminal element onto your property without risking the consequences.'

'Gregory,' said his wife sweetly, 'the summer fair has taken place there for over forty years, and the worst consequence we've had is one of the local drunks falling off a dodgem. What other kind of trouble are you anticipating?'

'Something serious, Perpetua,' he replied grumpily. 'Murder? I wouldn't put it past people like that.'

'Gregory, when we hear of someone being murdered down at Ratchetts Common, then we will do something about it. Until such time, I think we can leave well enough alone.'

'"Leave well enough alone"?' her husband echoed in doom-laden tones. 'Huh, what would have stopped the unions from taking over the country if Margaret Thatcher had "left well enough alone"?'

Having allowed him his ration of moaning, Perpetua Wintle felt able to move the conversation on. 'Oh, incidentally, I heard in the village shop that Highfield House is going to be occupied on a more permanent basis.'

'Oh? Has the place been sold?'

'No, but Major Bricket, the gentleman who's owned it all these years, is going to live permanently in Stunston Peveril.'

'Really? I've never met the fellow. Have I?' He usually relied on his wife's memory rather than his own.

'No, you haven't.'

'Have you?'

'No, Gregory. But, apparently, Major Bricket is "our kind of person".'

'Oh? Eton?'

'No.'

'Harrow?'

'No. Winchester.'

'Oh. Well, I suppose he just about scrapes in,' the Viscount conceded.

'I've invited him to the costume ball every year since he arrived in Stunston Peveril. But, so far, I have always received a punctiliously polite handwritten refusal. Work commitments. He travels abroad a lot, I gather.'

'Doing what?'

'I've no idea. This year, however,' the Viscountess went on, 'he has accepted the invitation.'

'Oh?' Gregory Wintle reached for the racing pages of his *Times*. 'Was at Winchester, eh?' he grunted. Without the security of knowing they went either to Eton or Harrow, how could he form a viable opinion of anyone? 'So, I can't imagine that this Major Bricket is going to impinge on our lives very much. Or on Stunston Peveril, come to that.'

Little did he know how inaccurate that remark would prove to be.

*

The same Wednesday lunchtime, in the Goat & Compasses, Stunston Peveril's only pub, the Major's plans to take up permanent residence in Highfield House were also being discussed. On a hot July day in one of Suffolk's most beautiful villages, business was brisk, but the landlord, Crocker Fosbury, prided himself on his skills of delegation. 'That's the art of management,' he would say with considerable frequency. 'Delegation. Get the right staff and you can be a proper landlord, welcoming customers and chatting with them. What people want when they come into a pub is chat.'

So, it never happened that Crocker Fosbury was too busy to have a chat. And the rumour round the village – that his skill of delegation relied on the fact that his wife, Mel, did all the work – was never voiced in his presence.

Because it was such a sunny day, most of the pub's customers wanted to be in the garden, so the landlord could have a nice little private session with his mates in the snug, which was known as 'Crocker's Corner'. There he could indulge his taste for chat, and the only work he did there was pulling pints for his cronies.

Also present that morning were his brother Derek, who was always there, and Bernard Lavoisier, owner of the circus currently occupying Ratchetts Common. (Or maybe he wasn't the owner any more . . . There had been a takeover of the business or something, but Crocker Fosbury hadn't got the details clear in his mind. This was partly because, as a conversationalist, he infinitely preferred talking to listening. The confusion may also have had something to do with Bernard Lavoisier's overdeveloped taste for alcohol, particularly brandy, which made his ramblings about the state of his business difficult to follow.)

'Crocker,' the circus owner slurred, 'you take my advice.' When he was performing as ring master, he had a marked French accent. The more he drank, the more this seemed to slip away in the direction of something nearer to Cockney. 'Crocker, don't do business with crooks. Doing business with crooks doesn't do you any good. And you know why? Because they're crooks.'

'That's true,' Derek Fosbury agreed. He was the least contentious person on God's earth. Rarely initiating conversation himself, he had a wide repertoire of responses to endorse anything anyone else said.

'And I've got involved with crooks,' Bernard Lavoisier maundered on. 'For some years, as I've been getting older . . . and I am, I am getting older . . . I've been trying to work out my . . . succession planning . . . and I've been looking for a partner . . . to share the load. But you don't want a partner who's a crook.'

'You're not wrong,' said Derek Fosbury.

His brother Crocker seemed to think he hadn't said enough for a while. 'I had a similar problem, way back, pub I was running in Ipswich. Assistant manager I had, he was a wrong 'un. Can't work with a wrong 'un.'

'You said it,' said Derek Fosbury.

'Crooks are despicable . . .' Bernard Lavoisier began.

But, having regained the conversational high ground, Crocker wasn't about to relinquish it. ''Nother thing I heard, Derek, is – Major Bricket's going to be living in Stunston Peveril, permanent like. Be nice to have him around.'

'Certainly will,' agreed Derek Fosbury.

'Not that we see that much of him when he is at home. In here for the occasional pint of Devil's Burp, but that's it. And nobody seems to know what he does for a living.'

'No, they don't,' said Derek Fosbury.

Bernard Lavoisier, apparently having given up being part of the conversation, was communing intimately with his brandy.

'Mind you,' the landlord went on, 'I know what the Major does.'

'Oh yes, Crocker? What's that then?' asked his brother.

'He's a hotel inspector. Spends his time going round the world, testing out the facilities of five-star hotels. Nice work if you can get it, eh?'

'Certainly is,' his brother agreed.

This view of what the Major did was, by Crocker Fosbury's standards, a modestly realistic one. Most unexplained things – the landlord normally reckoned – were caused by aliens.

At that moment, a young man in scruffy jeans and a T-shirt came into Crocker's Corner. He was probably late teens, small for his age, with dark eyes that looked jumpy and alert. The rest of him moved with the lethargy of adolescence. The landlord greeted him. 'Hi, Rod.'

'Hi, Crocker. Derek.' His accent suggested private education.

'Nice to see you, Rod,' said Derek with some warmth.

'You too, Derek. How's Bella?'

'Lovely as ever.'

'Of course. You got lucky there, Derek.'

'I did indeed. She's always been—'

But Crocker was not interested in hearing praise for

his sister-in-law. 'You don't know Bernard Lavoisier, do you, Rod?

'Lavoisier of the circus?'

'That's right.' But it was the landlord who replied rather than the man himself. Bernard was still more interested in his brandy than in being introduced to anyone.

'Pint of the old Devil's Burp, is it, Rod?'

'Please, Crocker.'

'And you can have it legal now.'

The boy blushed. He felt grown-up at eighteen and didn't want to be reminded of Crocker's former leniency about the legal drinking age.

'We was just talking about your boss,' said the landlord, as he started to pull the pint.

'Yes, we was,' Derek Fosbury agreed.

'Boss?' the young man echoed. 'I haven't got a boss. To have a boss you have to have a job. Which at the moment, sadly, I don't.'

'No? I thought you was meant to be looking after Major Bricket's garden.'

'Oh yeah, well, I know I'm meant to, but I only, like, do it when I know he's going to be back in Stunston Peveril.'

'Well, he is going to be back in Stunston Peveril.'

'What?'

'For good.'

'You're having a laugh.'

'No way, Rod,' said Crocker.

'No way,' his brother agreed.

'When's he coming back?' asked Rod.

'This afternoon.'

'Holy Moses! Hold the Devil's Burp, Crocker. I must get back and mow his lawn!'

Suddenly less lethargic, the young man rushed out of the Goat & Compasses.

In the Green Lotus, Stunston Peveril's – rather daringly different – Thai restaurant, Nga Luong was making spring rolls. It was a task which she had performed so often, she could have done it with her eyes closed. Taking out the prepared wrappers, grating the ginger, slicing the shiitake mushrooms and the water chestnuts, cutting the tinned bamboo shoots into matchsticks, shredding the cavolo nero. With that done, she then added the secret ingredients and sauces which made her spring rolls distinctive, ingredients that had the Green Lotus customers drooling and demanding the one thing she would never give them – her recipe.

The difference from ordinary spring rolls came from Nga's heritage. She originated from Vietnam rather than Thailand, but, an eternally practical woman, had decided her potential clientele might find a Thai restaurant more appealing than a Vietnamese one.

The English middle class of Suffolk were not highly attuned to such nuances. Though there was pressure in the right-on media to respect individual ethnicity, the residents of Stunston Peveril were a bit hazy about the national differences among people from the East. So long as they were enjoying their food, they weren't too bothered whether its origin was Thai or Vietnamese. Nga Luong, an easy-going woman secure in her own identity, was amused rather than offended by their ignorance.

She knew she had witnessed more of the world and its dangers than the residents of Stunston Peveril ever would.

Nga Luong quietly enjoyed playing up to the prejudices of the English middle classes. They were not guilty of cultural appropriation, more of complete lack of interest in the cultures of other countries. Many of them had done luxury package tours to Thailand, incorporating five-star hotels, visits to Bangkok's Grand Palace, Temple of the Golden Buddha and floating market, as well as a dinner cruise on the Chao Phraya River.

They had then flown to Phuket, where they spent the rest of their fortnight draped over loungers on beaches (only interrupted by a full-day excursion to the iconic Phi Phi Islands).

So, they knew all about Thailand.

As to Vietnam, some denizens of Stunston Peveril had investigated going there to see the massive temple complex of Angkor Wat (before they discovered it was in Cambodia). So, they reckoned they knew about Vietnam too.

This vagueness about foreign cultures manifested itself in another way in the Green Lotus Restaurant. Quite frequently, their experience of Asian cuisine having been mostly in Chinese restaurants, customers nearing the end of their meals would ask the waitresses whether they'd be getting fortune cookies. The first time this happened, the English waitresses didn't know how to answer and took the problem to Nga Luong in the kitchen.

She, fully aware that fortune cookies had nothing to do with the Orient and had been invented in California in the early years of the twentieth century, solemnly went out into the restaurant and addressed the table who had raised the question. Maintaining a pose of complete seriousness, she announced, in a much heavier accent than she usually used, 'The tradition of the fortune cookie in

Thailand is different from other countries. Diners get the fortune, but not the cookie.'

Seeing the confused faces, she elaborated, 'If diners in a Thai restaurant ask for a fortune cookie, it is the custom for the proprietor to tell them their fortune.'

'What?' asked one of the group. 'You produce a piece of paper with the fortune written on it?'

'No,' said Nga Luong. 'The proprietor just tells them their fortune by speaking.'

'All right. So, what's mine?'

Nga Luong had closed her eyes and furrowed her brow, as if communicating with some unseen power. Then she proclaimed, in sombre tones, 'When even a small frog jumps into a pond, there will be a splash.'

The diners had been very impressed. They were vaguely aware of the concept of Eastern wisdom. They had seen cartoons of gurus dispensing abstruse thoughts from the tops of mountains. They had heard of philosophers, from Confucius onwards, giving rules for life in gnomic utterances. And they appreciated the fact that Nga Luong had shared her mystic gift with them.

The customer who had asked the original question interpreted her words to mean that even the smallest happening will trigger other events. As a result, he changed his plans for the evening ahead. After the dinner, his intention had been to go to visit his mistress. But the fortune cookie's gem of Eastern wisdom persuaded him to go back instead to his wife, to whom he was never again unfaithful.

The news of Nga Luong's mystical powers did not take long to spread throughout Stunston Peveril. It became the habit of the more superstitious residents, when faced by some social or moral dilemma, to go and have a meal at the Green Lotus Restaurant. When they had finished their dessert, they would ask the waitress for a fortune cookie. Nga Luong would be ceremoniously summoned from the kitchen and articulate the latest words of ancient enlightenment that she had just thought of.

She was careful never to give direct advice. She took care that her pearls of sagacity were capable of more than one interpretation, and the customers with dilemmas always interpreted them as encouragement to follow the course that they had already decided to take.

Delighted by the success of the game, Nga Luong mentally dubbed herself 'The Human Fortune Cookie'. The availability of oriental mysticism did no harm to the numbers of locals booking at the Green Lotus Restaurant.

The English frequently described people from the Far East as 'inscrutable'. Nga Luong could do inscrutability with the best of them. And no one knew that, as she dispensed her gnomic maxims, behind her inscrutable exterior she was sending them up rotten.

A ting from her mobile not only brought her back to the present and the manufacture of spring rolls, it also notified her she had a text message. She wiped her hands on kitchen roll before picking up the phone.

The text read: 'I will be arriving at the house later this afternoon. I'm occupied this evening, but thereafter will you be up for some cooking? MB.'

Nga Luong smiled. Life could never be dull when the Major was around.

Major Bricket felt good being back, wearing his familiar tweed sports jacket, in his familiar red 1976 MG Midget.

Not just good at being back in the car, but good at being back in England. The travels which had taken him all over the world for the past three decades had not been without their excitements, but it was time for a change. He was careful not, even to himself, to use the words 'complete retirement', but he looked forward to whatever his new life might bring. And he felt confident that it would be different.

He turned the open red sports car into Stunston Peveril and was warmed by the familiar sights of the village. He had enjoyed happy times there. Sad ones too, but he didn't dwell on those. There were few places he had ever been where all of his memories had been untainted by sadness. And, though much of the Major's training had been in hiding his feelings, that did not mean he hadn't got any. He just found he could suppress them by being relentlessly active.

As he passed, he looked along the unchanging parade of the High Street . . . the Gingham Tea Shop . . . the Green Lotus Thai Restaurant . . . Cosy Collectibles with its usual window display of things he'd never give house room to. (That didn't mean, however, that he'd never been in the shop. It was the closest place to his home where he could buy batteries. And it seemed discourteous to the owner, Rhona, if batteries were all he bought. So, at Highfield House, he had a small collection of figurines of the Royal Family with nodding heads. They were kept securely in a locked drawer where no visitors to the house might ever see them. Though the Major appeared stern, he could be quite a softie at times.)

As he drove past the Goat & Compasses, he thought he could do worse than end the day having a couple of pints there. Such indulgences, of course, now became possible for a retired person. But, even as the idea arrived, the Major reminded himself that he was otherwise committed that evening. The Fincham Abbey Costume Ball.

He stopped the Midget on the road outside Highfield House and opened the gates. A high summer afternoon in an English village – what could be more appealing?

Clicking the gates closed behind him, he drove the car to a standstill on the semicircle of gravel in front of the garage. He noticed that the garden had not been watered as regularly as it should have been. And the lawn gave the impression of having been mowed hastily. He'd have to have a word with Rod Enright about that. But he didn't feel angry. If anything, he felt protective. He knew doing gardening was not a natural fit for the boy. Maybe there was something else to which he might be better suited . . .?

Major Bricket was in no hurry to get into the house. A greater attraction for him lay in the shed at the end of the garden. But, a man of strict priorities, he would park the car first.

He pressed the remote on his ring of keys and the garage door lifted up and over. He was about to drive the Midget in when he noticed that there was something on the floor in front of him. He got out of the car to inspect.

Spreadeagled on the cement floor of the garage lay a dead body.

The corpse was dressed in a clown's costume. Bald plastic cranium with side-tufts of ropey orange hair. Red jacket, too long. Black-and-white check trousers suspended from elastic braces to a hooped waistband. Shoes three foot long pointing outwards in a strange semaphore.

Well, he's really turned his toes up, thought the Major, inappropriately.

Around the man's neck, an iron bar had been twisted. The clown had had his last laugh.

2

The Costume Ball

Given his background, of course Major Bricket knew the correct protocol to be followed upon the discovery of a dead body. But, also given his background, there was no way he was going to contact the proper authorities before he had made his own examination of the crime scene.

This involved a close inspection of the corpse, conducted without any physical contact. A young man, probably early twenties, slight, not tall. Tattoos on his forearms should make him easy to identify. The Major took relevant photographs with his rather superior phone camera.

Scrutiny of the front garden left him in no doubt that the murder had taken place elsewhere. Tyre tracks in the gravel suggested someone had driven a fairly heavy van into his property and dragged the corpse out and over the gravel to its resting place in the garage.

Two other deductions arose from his examination of the crime scene. First, the clown suit had not been designed for the dead person who was wearing it. The fabric was loose over the small, wiry body and the feet had been stuffed inadequately into the long shoes.

Second, the iron bar twisted round the victim's neck was not what had killed him. A surprisingly small trace of blood was visible on the cement floor beneath his head. The cause of death had been a bullet to the back of the neck.

The Major, obviously, knew that the method was used as a form of execution in China and in gangland killings all over the world, but he did not allow his mind to extrapolate anything from that. Long experience had inured him to the dangers of jumping to conclusions.

Leaving the Midget where he'd stopped it, he took out his luggage and entered Highfield House for the first time in many months. The weekly cleaners had been in two days before and everything looked immaculate.

Major Bricket left his bags in the hall, went through into the sitting room, and poured himself a healthy tumbler of Scotch. The fridge had been switched off during his long absence, so he didn't bother to go to the kitchen for ice. Postings abroad where it wasn't available had got him used to doing without.

He enjoyed a long swallow, took his phone out of his tweed jacket pocket, and did the proper thing. Called the police to tell them about the corpse in his garage.

In a long and varied life, Major Bricket had noticed a tendency for members of certain professions to embrace its stereotype. Playing rugby at school (where he had been a nippy and elusive scrum half), he had heard the sports masters shouting outdated encouragements they had heard from their own sports masters. He had been examined by doctors who disguised their callowness by dressing in the pin-striped suits of a previous generation.

And he recognised the same syndrome being exemplified by Detective Inspector Pritchett who, having summoned the Scene of Crime team to conduct their procedures in the Highfield House garage and garden, was now questioning its owner in his sitting room.

The Inspector was a heavyset man, probably in his late fifties. He wore a sports jacket which had been long moulded to his contours, and fawn moleskin trousers abandoned many years before by straight creases. His manner was almost ponderous, a style borrowed from a number of slow-witted television detectives.

Major Bricket suspected that this was a front, carefully designed to put interviewees at their ease, to make criminals feel they'd got lucky, being questioned by such an unimaginative bonehead. Accordingly, he was on his guard.

He was also aware of the old crime fiction trope that the person who discovers the body immediately becomes the first suspect. He also knew that he could quickly be exonerated from any accusation. His arrival at Heathrow earlier in the day had been heavily documented. As was his custom, he had taken a cab from the airport to the private garage in Staines where he left the Midget when he was working abroad. His presence there could be vouched for by the garage owner, a former colleague. And there were enough CCTV cameras on the roads between Staines and Stunston Peveril to make a record of his journey. Nobody arriving at Highfield House when he did would have had time to murder the man in the clown suit.

But Major Bricket did not offer this explanation to Pritchett. He knew the Inspector wouldn't have had time yet to corroborate the details of his journey. And to offer explanations before they were asked for always looked like covering up guilt. He allowed his interrogator to proceed at his own pace.

'Well, Major,' Detective Inspector Pritchett began weightily, 'you could not identify the body you found in your garage?'

'I have never seen him before.'

'And, Major Bricket, a very obvious question, but one I have to ask in the circumstances ... Do you have any enemies?'

'Good heavens, no. Well, I may have annoyed one of my classmates at prep school by helping myself to his chewing gum, but that's about it.' The answer was offered in a jocular manner, as if such a thought had never before entered the Major's head. Even though the bit about his having no enemies was a blatant lie.

'So, you can think of no reason why your garage should be chosen as a repository for a corpse?'

'None at all, I'm afraid, Inspector.'

Ponderously, and once more living up to the stereotype he was projecting, Detective Inspector Pritchett took a reporter's notebook out of his side pocket. He reached inside his jacket for a ballpoint pen which he clicked on. (At least he hadn't taken out the stub of a pencil and licked it.)

These rituals completed, he addressed his interviewee more formally, 'I gather, Major Bricket, that you have just returned from abroad ...?'

'Yes, I was in Croatia.'

'And was that business or pleasure?'

'Pleasure, sheer pleasure, Inspector.'

'And, had it been business, might I ask what your business might be?'

The Major spread his arms wide. 'I am gloriously retired.'

'Ah. Croatia ...' the policeman ruminated. 'That's where they've just had that hostage crisis, isn't it?'

A blank look. 'Sorry, when I'm on holiday, I avoid reading the papers and online news.'

'Nasty business. Three heavily armed terrorists took over a bank, half a dozen bank staff taken hostage. Usual threats ... you know, shooting the hostages one by one if their demands weren't met. Very ugly.'

'Ugly indeed. Is it still going on?' asked the Major innocently.

'No. Satisfactory conclusion, I'm glad to say. Hostages released; terrorists arrested. No bloodshed. But there were times when it looked as if it was going to end very differently.'

'Ah.' The Major's tone implied that, though regretting the unpleasantness, he didn't have a great deal of interest in this recently resolved crisis.

But Detective Inspector Pritchett wasn't ready to abandon the subject quite yet. 'It happened in Dubrovnik,' he said.

'I wouldn't know about that. I was miles away from the capital. Croatia's a big country.'

'Yes. I've never had the pleasure of going there.'

'You've missed some charming people. And some beautiful scenery.'

'And is that why you were there, Major? For the scenery?'

'Partly. But, also, I have a layman's interest in church architecture.' He gestured to his bookshelf, which contained a section of books on the subject. 'Croatia boasts some wonderful pre-Romanesque churches.'

'Really?'

'Many of them,' Major Bricket enthused, 'show distinct Frankish and Byzantine influences.'

'Ah, do they?' said Detective Inspector Pritchett, making the decision that enough had now been said about Croatia. 'Are you aware, Major, that there is a circus currently occupying Ratchetts Common?'

'I hadn't really thought about it but, yes, that would make sense. I know there always is a circus in Stunston Peveril the same week as the costume ball up at Fincham Abbey.'

'Which does, at least in one respect, make my job easier.'

'Sorry, Inspector, I don't follow.'

The policeman chuckled. 'Well, we don't have to look far to find out where the clown's costume came from, do we?'

The Major shook his head in admiration. 'Remarkable. I'm sure it's insights like that which have made you such a success in your chosen profession, Inspector.'

Detective Inspector Pritchett accepted the compliment with a self-congratulatory smile, but his joviality was short-lived. His face took on a look almost of suspicion as he asked, 'Presumably, Major, I could check that you came straight here from the airport this afternoon?'

He went through the routine. 'I picked up my car from a garage in Staines, chatted to the owner there, then drove straight here. Thus, if that were the direction in which your mind was moving, I wouldn't have had time to commit a murder, dress the corpse in a clown suit and deposit him in my own garage.'

'That was not the direction in which my mind was

moving,' the Inspector lied. 'But I do have to ask, Major Bricket, do you have plans to travel abroad again in the near future?'

'No, Inspector. As I said, I am gloriously retired. For the near future at least, my horizon will be what I can see from the windows of this house ... Well, maybe a little further than that. My horizon must, of necessity, include in its scope the Goat & Compasses pub in the village, And the Green Lotus Thai Restaurant.

'But have no fear, Inspector. If your investigations prove that I am responsible for the unfortunate corpse in my garage, you will not have to enlist Interpol to find me for the purposes of arrest. From this day forward, I am a permanent resident of Stunston Peveril.'

For many people, a costume ball would necessitate a visit to a fancy-dress shop or endless searching online, agonising over whether what's on offer would fit and what kind of quality fabrics it would be made of. Major Bricket had no such problems.

There was a conventional wardrobe in one of the Highfield House spare rooms. The rail was hung with an array of elderly suits, and no one would have suspected what lay behind them. No access to Narnia was on offer (a source of relief to people who found Christian allegory wearisome), but there was a sliding wooden door which revealed another deep cupboard behind.

Here were arrayed a variety of costumes which the Major had needed over the years. Military uniforms, some British but most representing other countries' armies. A selection of business suits, ranging from the sedately conventional to the downright flashy. Any number of shabby jeans and T-shirts. And a range of ethnic apparel.

Major Bricket knew exactly what he was looking for. Something light for a summer evening. He removed from its hangers the full-length white tunic known as a *thobe*. He also collected the square of fabric called a *gutra*, which would cover his head and be held in place by the black goat-hair ring of an *agal*. Finally, he added the *sirwal*, a pair of short white harem pants.

For the Wintles' costume ball, the Major had decided to go Arab.

In common with many English country houses, there was a lot that needed doing at Fincham Abbey. Routine maintenance had been at a minimum, a direct consequence of lack of staff, and of the Viscount's invariably finding builders' estimates excessive. Guests staying for long weekends with the Wintles were accustomed to find corners of their bedrooms where cobwebs had been allowed to proliferate, perhaps for centuries. Windows fitted badly and carpets, of which there were few, looked threadbare. The water that trickled reluctantly out of the bathroom taps was brown. When the heating came on, it did a reasonable impression of an old man with asthma.

But on the night of the costume ball, none of these shortcomings was in evidence. The event started at eight o'clock, on an English summer evening that could have been a finalist in a Best English Summer Evening competition. Drinks – champagne, obviously – were served in the abbey's courtyard, bedizened by strings of lights. As the shadows lengthened, the centre of activities moved indoors to what, pre-Reformation when the building was still in ecclesiastical ownership, had been the refectory.

In the nineteenth century, that rarity – a Viscount Wintle with a lot of money – had had that space refurbished and redesignated as 'the Ballroom'. There it was that the drinking continued, and lavish canapés were served to the guests. It was there, too, that a function band played a mix of waltzes and foxtrots, interspersed with what Gregory Wintle called 'more modern stuff', some of which was as recent as the Beatles.

The array of costumes the ball featured was impressive. As Major Bricket arrived at Fincham Abbey, he found himself surrounded by characters from every nationality and century. There was the usual ration of knights in armour and nuns, a sprinkling of cavemen and crinoline ladies, a couple of pharaohs and even one of their mummies. Soldiers ranged from hussars to Household Cavalry. Hippies exchanged thoughts with superheroes (that didn't take long), and the wildlife represented encompassed frogs and foxes.

Major Bricket did not feel out of place dressed as a sheikh. But then the Major never felt out of place in any milieu. At the entrance to the courtyard, he took a glass of champagne from a tray borne by one of the Fincham Abbey staff. His favourite tipple was whisky, which he drank with meals as well as before and after them. But he had learnt over the years of his career to be infinitely adaptable, and he could always tolerate a good champagne.

He was greeted at the wide doorway to the courtyard by Perpetua, Viscountess Wintle. When he'd identified himself, she said, 'Oh, so delighted you could make it this year, Major. I believe you've been abroad every other time we've invited you to the ball.'

'Yes, Lady Wintle. And it's something I regret deeply. The Fincham Abbey Costume Balls are legendary. I have been kept away by the demands of work, I'm afraid. But now I have retired and will be able to spend more time enjoying the delights of Stunston Peveril.'

'It will be a great pleasure to see more of you, Major Bricket.' Perpetua had, needless to say, been beautifully brought up. She could have represented England in the Olympic Small Talk Competition. 'I apologise that Gregory is not here to greet you. He is yet again going through his collection of this year's costumes, deciding which one suits him best. He will be making his appearance at the ball later.'

'I look forward to meeting him.'

Viscountess Wintle, acknowledging the end of their conversation with a polite nod of her head, turned to meet her next guest, who was dressed as a kangaroo and announced himself, in a thick Australian accent, as 'Lord Piers Goodruff. You didn't recognise me in the roo kit, did you, Perp?'

It struck Major Bricket how convenient a costume ball was for people who were bad at remembering names. Since only a few guests were recognisable, with others hidden behind masks and headdresses, it was reasonable that everyone had to announce themselves. It saved a lot of potential embarrassment, while at the same time avoiding the awkwardness of people standing around not sure who to start a conversation with. Everyone started on more or less the same footing. With the costumes themselves as a ready-made topic for discussion.

The Major was not a man to feel awkward in any social setting. He had acquitted himself in far more challenging environments than the Fincham Abbey Costume Ball. But, since he knew who Lord Piers Goodruff was, he thought he might as well start a conversation with the newest arrival.

The sheikh offered a hand to the kangaroo. 'Good evening, Lord Goodruff. You do not know me. My name is Major Bricket. But I did just want to say how much I've appreciated the way the political stance of the *Daily Signal* has subtly changed since you took over ownership.'

Many dealings with foreign dignitaries had taught the Major the age-old lesson: it never hurts to start a conversation with a little flattery. And, though he couldn't see the kangaroo's face, the creature's body language expressed self-congratulatory satisfaction at his approach.

'Yes,' it replied. 'Takes an Aussie to tell the Poms where their political sympathies should lie.'

'Exactly.' So practised was the Major's response that the hearer might well think it was an endorsement of his political stance. Only the speaker knew how far from the truth that was.

'It seems you're rarely out of the news these days, Lord Goodruff.'

The kangaroo shrugged. 'Goes with the territory, mate. If you're a media mogul, I'm afraid everyone wants a piece of you.'

'I have only to open the financial pages to read of some new company you're buying.'

'Got to diversify, Major. Keep your arse covered, prepared for attacks from every direction.'

'Yes, of course.'

As he spoke, Major Bricket was asking himself quite how Lord Piers Goodruff came to be attending the Fincham

Abbey Costume Ball. The peer had global interests – a media empire built up by canny purchase of newspapers and television stations, a hotel chain, investments in foreign airlines, football teams in the UK and the States. There were few pies into which his grubby fingers had not been inserted.

And yet, though he had taken UK citizenship, cosied up to governments and effectively gate-crashed English society, the Australian did not really fit into the Old Etonian coterie with which Viscount Wintle liked to surround himself. But again, the Major concluded, it was probably a case of money talking. In this instance, like its owner, in a very loud voice.

By now the noble Lord, deciding that there was nothing useful for him to be gained from their dialogue, had wandered off. The Major, always a man with his own agenda, also wandered off. Into the interior of Fincham Abbey.

It was a habit he had developed through his career, the restless thirst for information. To be in an unfamiliar building without exploring it a little went against Major Bricket's every instinct. For one thing, he always wanted to know where the exits were.

So, he just took a short tour of Fincham Abbey's ground floor. If anyone questioned where the sheikh was going, he had the all-purpose excuse of being in search of the gents. But, in the event, the abbey staff were far too busy to take any notice of him.

What struck the Major, apart from the general tackiness of everything, was the number of paintings hung on the interior walls, particularly in the Great Hall. Art was not one of his special subjects, but he knew enough about it to recognise, if not the written signatures, the signature style of some major British artists from the seventeenth to the nineteenth centuries.

He did not find it odd. It was endearingly characteristic of the country's aristocracy, rather in the way they prided themselves on wearing threadbare clothes. To live in a state of shabbiness while having one's walls covered with valuable and undoubtedly saleable artwork had a charm that was quintessentially English.

The Major was also struck by an anomaly among the paintings. All were ill-lit but, though most were festooned with cobwebs and dust, a few appeared to be marginally cleaner than the rest. He looked at those more closely than he did the others.

As no one had taken much notice of his entry to the house, nobody took much notice of his leaving it and returning to the party. The Major looked around the champagne-quaffing crowd for a familiar unmasked face. He was rewarded by the sight of a Madame de Pompadour, whose overstated white wig sat atop the recognisable features of Venetia Clothbury. For a moment, the Major questioned why the octogenarian should be on the Fincham Abbey Costume Ball invitation list, before recalling that her husband, Sydney, had been an Old Etonian. Another example of Viscount Wintle sticking to his tribe.

The Major greeted the widow with his customary punctiliousness. Because his sheikh costume left his face uncovered, she had no difficulty in recognising him.

'Ah, Major Bricket,' she boomed at her customary

volume. Fortunately, the ambient noise was already so loud that she did not disturb any of the other guests. 'I gather exciting things have been happening up at Highfield House.'

'It depends how you define "exciting",' came the cautious reply. He knew that news spread quickly in Stunston Peveril, but surely no one yet had heard about the clown's corpse in his garage.

That anxiety was quickly allayed, as Venetia Clothbury said, 'I'm talking about the news that you are to become a permanent resident there.'

'Oh yes. I've been looking forward to this for a long time. Extended leisure in Stunston Peveril – what more could one ask for?'

'So, you are fully retired now, are you, Major?'

'Absolutely.'

'Well, you know, there are vacancies on the Village Committee. I myself am a past chairperson. And now you have more time on your hands . . .'

'I'm afraid I've never been much of a committee person, Venetia. I lack the grasp of detail which you clearly have.'

She accepted the compliment with a gracious smile, knowing it was no more than her due. 'The Village Committee does some very important work.'

'I'm sure it does.'

'And organises interesting events.'

'Really?'

'Oh yes. For instance, tomorrow evening at eight o'clock in the village hall, there's a discussion, which I am chairing, on the question, "Who Is Responsible for Potholes?"'

'Ah.'

'Perhaps you'd like to come along, Major . . .?'

'I'll have to check the diary,' he said charmingly, as if it was something he genuinely intended to do.

'Of course. Now you've retired, you know, there has been considerable speculation in the village as to what you have actually retired *from*.'

If Venetia Clothbury thought she was going to get the answer that easily, she had underestimated the opposition. 'There's always conjecture about everything in a small village,' the Major commented smoothly before moving the conversation on. 'As a prominent member of Stunston Peveril society, you've been to these costume balls before, I am sure, Venetia.'

'Oh yes, indeed. My late husband, Sydney, was at Eton with the Viscount.'

'Of course.'

She made one more attempt. 'As I said, there has been a lot of speculation about what your job was, Major . . .?'

'And, as I said, that's inevitable in a small village,' he countered.

'Though,' Venetia Clothbury went on, mysteriously, 'of course, I actually know what you do – or should I say "did".'

'Really?'

A conspiratorial nose-tap. 'If I were to say that the Royal Family's foreign tours will not be as well organised in the future as they have been in the past . . . would I be far off the mark?'

It did not seem gracious to tell her exactly how far off the mark she was, so the Major just said, with an engaging shrug, 'Ridiculous that I should think I could pull the wool over your eyes, Venetia.'

Madame de Pompadour smiled knowingly. She'd have something to tell that Mollie Greenford when they next met in the Gingham Tea Shop.

Major Bricket knew he would have to be on his guard. There had been a police presence at Highfield House. Venetia Clothbury had not heard that on the village grapevine yet – probably because she had been busy getting herself into her elaborate costume. But soon all of Stunston Peveril would have shared the news. Only a matter of time before everyone knew about the murder. And before the consequent tsunami of speculation was unleashed.

His own speculations were interrupted by the band ceasing to play their version of 'Yesterday' and segueing into a fanfare. From the top of the steps which fronted Fincham Abbey's main doors, Viscount Wintle irrupted onto the scene.

He was dressed in a clown costume.

3

A Visit to the Circus

As Major Bricket anticipated, although Venetia Clothbury had been unaware of events at Highfield House, the variety of police vehicles gathered outside had not gone unnoticed by the rest of the village. The Stunston Peveril grapevine – disseminated by the local WhatsApp group, phone calls and old-fashioned chatting over garden fences – had quickly generated an inundation of conjecture. By the following morning, the Tuesday, every resident had a theory as to what had happened.

In the Gingham Tea Shop, its owner Elvira Finchcombe shared her views with all the coffee drinkers who wanted to listen – and, because her voice was rather loud, with all who didn't want to listen, as well. An unexploded World War II bomb, she asserted, had been found in the garden of Highfield House. That was why all the police vehicles were there. She went on to share her certainty that specialist bomb-disposal experts were, even at that moment, on their way to Stunston Peveril to arrange a controlled explosion.

Rhona in Cosy Collectibles was in no doubt it was illegal immigrants. Though most of them entered the country on the south coast, she was convinced it was only a matter of time before they realised the advantages of the long East Anglian shoreline. She'd had a couple in the shop only a week before who spoke limited English and didn't recognise who was the model for the Winston Churchill Nodding Head Figurine (one of her most popular lines – to his shame, Major Bricket had once bought one on the search for batteries). That was what gave the couple away. Rhona felt sure they were camping out at Highfield House, and all the police activity was in the cause of arresting them.

Lena who cleaned at the vicarage was not backward in sharing her opinions with the vicar's wife (much of whose life, because of her husband's calling, had been occupied by listening to people telling her things that didn't interest her). In Lena's opinion, Highfield House had been infiltrated by a demonic cult, whose practices included human sacrifice. An escaped cult member had alerted the police to these atrocities.

Dierdre in the Post Office didn't subscribe to any of these views. She knew that Stunston Peveril was situated at a place where two highly significant ley lines intersected. Beneath Highfield House was an ancient chapel, hidden in which was a casket containing a piece of the True Cross, which had been buried there by the Knights Templar. Someone must have tried to break into the chapel and, according to the vows they had taken, the Knights Templar had killed the desecrator of their hallowed sanctum. It was the discovery of the heretic's hideously mangled body which had brought the police to Stunston Peveril.

Meanwhile, in the Goat & Compasses, Crocker Fosbury would not have listened to such superstitious nonsense.

He felt pretty sure that the disturbing events at Highfield House were the work of aliens.

Major Bricket woke later than usual that Tuesday. His custom was to spring out of bed on the dot of six thirty, but that morning it was nine. This was not due to excess at the costume ball – the Major was punctilious about controlling his drinking – but to jetlag. It was only the previous day that he had landed at Heathrow after a series of long international flights, culminating in the one from Croatia.

He shaved, showered and breakfasted with his usual efficiency. He then went out to check what police activity there was in his garage and surrounding area. On arriving the previous afternoon, his first intended destination had been the garden shed, but the discovery of the clown corpse had frustrated that plan. The spread of policemen, incident tape and forensic equipment on the Tuesday morning suggested it would still be a while before he could get in there.

There was stuff he needed to do on the laptop, though. Reports and things. Though Major Bricket was now officially retired, there was still paperwork to tidy up.

He also rang Nga Luong to make arrangements for that evening.

It was after twelve by the time Major Bricket had cleared the most urgent emails. Perfect timing for a pint of Devil's Burp at the Goat & Compasses.

Another lovely day, so once again most of the pub's customers – many in Stunston Peveril for the afternoon performance of Lavoisier's Circus – were sitting outside.

From long habit, the Major made his way to 'Crocker's Corner' where, as he could have predicted, the landlord was pontificating to his cronies.

It was the same two cronies as the day before: his brother and Bernard Lavoisier. The Major already knew Derek, and the introduction to the circus owner was quickly made. Fresh pints of Devil's Burp were quickly pulled, too.

'Funny, Major,' said Crocker, 'we was just talking about you.'

'Yes, we was,' Derek agreed. 'Only yesterday.'

'Oh?' Major Bricket smiled. 'Nothing bad, I hope?'

'No, no. Nothing bad,' Crocker assured him. 'Just, people couldn't help observing . . . been a lot of police cars up at your place.'

'Oh yes,' came the easy response. The details would inevitably come out in time, but there was no need to mention the word 'murder' yet. 'People had been trespassing at Highfield House while I was away.' No need to mention that one trespasser was found dead in the garage, either. Or that the other trespasser might well have murdered him.

'It's always a risk leaving a place empty for a long time,' said Derek Fosbury. Which was quite a long sentence for him.

'I thought young Rod was meant to be keeping an eye on things for you while you was away,' said Crocker.

'Just on the garden.'

'So, you don't think he might have let some of his mates in, you know, for like a party or—?'

'No, I don't think that's at all likely,' the Major interrupted smoothly. 'Rod's a good lad and I trust him implicitly.'

The landlord wasn't convinced. 'Well, that's your decision...'

For once, Derek didn't concur. 'Major's right, Crocker. There's no harm in that boy and he's always—'

Predictably, he was cut off by his brother. 'I never quite trust Rod.'

Major Bricket leapt to the defence. 'Well, I do. Boy's had a tough life. Losing his mother so young.'

'That's true,' said the landlord grudgingly.

'Yes, it certainly is,' his brother agreed, with more enthusiasm.

Crocker smiled nostalgically. 'She was a lovely woman, Sylvia.'

'She was,' Derek agreed. 'Bella always said she—'

'Lovely woman,' Crocker repeated, again automatically speaking over his brother.

'Certainly,' the Major agreed. 'Lovely woman. Did you ever meet Rod's father?'

Crocker grimaced. 'Jim Enright? Nasty bit of work.'

'Nasty bit of work,' Derek agreed.

'Left Sylvia in the lurch, just like that. Walked out on her and Rod. Mel – that's my missus...'

'I know Mel, Crocker.'

'Course you do, Major.'

'Creator of the best fish pie in the known universe.'

'Nice of you to say so. Anyway, Mel reckons it was the strain of how Jim behaved to her that brought on Sylvia's cancer.'

'Possible.'

'Very quick it was. Six weeks after the diagnosis, she was gone. Leaving Rod to fend for himself.'

'I know. Which is why,' the Major went on, 'I have a lot

of time for the boy. I've a feeling he has a bright future. Just hasn't found his proper niche in life yet.'

'You may be right,' said Crocker.

'You are right,' said Derek, sounding more optimistic than his brother about the boy's chances of coming good.

Surprisingly – and uncharacteristically – Derek continued speaking. 'I saw a lot of Rod just after Sylvia died. Living so close to them, we did what we could to help, but—'

'There was an article in the *Sunday Express* at the weekend,' said Crocker. He was so used to ignoring anything his brother said, it was as if he didn't recognise that Derek was speaking. And, like some automatic toy, when Crocker opened his mouth, Derek shut his. 'Piece about aliens landing in Suffolk. I think it's probably true. Would explain some very strange things that have been going on locally. And I know a lot of people don't believe in aliens. But what I'd say to them is: if the aliens didn't exist, why would there be so many articles written about them?'

This was a discussion that the Major did not wish to pursue. He wanted to get back to what Derek had been saying about Rod Enright. But, before he could speak, another voice chipped in.

'Fill her up, could you?'

Bernard Lavoisier had so far had little to contribute to the conversation. His brandy had far more appeal than Stunston Peveril gossip. He drew Crocker Fosbury's attention to the fact that he needed a refill. While the landlord topped up his balloon, Major Bricket enquired affably as to how the circus was going.

'Don't ask me,' came the reply. Bernard Lavoisier did not even attempt to make his accent French. 'The daughter's in charge now. Camille, she runs it. If you want to know how the circus is going, you'd better ask her.'

'You know, I might just do that.'

'I hope you find her in a better mood than I did this morning. She's no friend of mine, that daughter. You know the latest thing she's done? She's only stopped me from being ring master. In my own circus! Now she insists on doing that. She's the one in the middle of the ring in the red tailcoat – specially designed, of course, by some posh London designer. Hate to think what it cost. I'd stand up to her and get my job back . . . if I thought there was any point.'

He took a lugubrious swallow of brandy. 'But the whole shooting match is going to hell in a handcart, so I may as well just let it happen. As for Camille's chances of saving Lavoisier's Circus, she hasn't got a snowball's in hell.

'And her temper hasn't been improved by having police all round the place this morning.'

The Major was instantly alert. 'At the circus?'

'Yes.'

It figured. Detective Inspector Pritchett had said he was going to focus his inquiries there. 'Mr Lavoisier,' Major Bricket asked, 'do you know if the police reached any conclusions?'

'No idea. I've been in here from the minute Crocker opened up.'

'Ah. I was thinking . . .' said the Major, deceptively casual, 'I haven't been to the circus since I was in short trousers. Always loved it back then. Had a grandfather who used to take me. When's your next performance?'

Lavoisier looked blearily at his watch. 'Half past two it'll be.'

'And am I likely to be able to get a ticket?'

'You'll get a ticket,' said the doom-laden proprietor. 'No problem about that.'

The Major checked his own watch. 'Excellent. Time for another pint of the old Devil's Burp – and whatever the rest of you are having. And tell me, Crocker, has Mel still got that world-beating fish pie on the lunch menu?'

The fish pie proving as excellent as it had been in his recollection, and the Devil's Burp just as good, Major Bricket felt full of bonhomie as he wandered from the Goat & Compasses down to Ratchetts Common, arriving shortly after two. He noticed with interest a couple of police cars parked near the circus entrance.

There was no queue at the box office and the choice of seats he was offered implied the afternoon's performance was not a sell-out. But the number of families picnicking with excited children on the greensward suggested the Big Top wouldn't be completely empty either. On the area in front of the entrance were a couple of mini-carousels, a dodgems layout, and a helter-skelter. Nearby were coconut shy, whack-a-mole and candy floss stalls. All were doing a thriving trade.

Major Bricket would claim no magic powers of invisibility, but he did have a great skill in going unnoticed. This ability had been a necessity, which he had developed throughout his professional life. The secret, however alien the environment in which he found himself, was always to look purposeful, as if he knew exactly where he was heading. Nothing raises suspicions more than someone wandering around, appearing to have no destination.

So, he looked purposeful when he moved round the

back of the Big Top to the area where the circus staff's caravans were corralled. Everyone else looked purposeful there, too. They were, after all, about to put on a show. There were predictable smells of horse manure, baked dust and diesel from the playground engines.

Seeing a couple of rather furtive-looking men ahead of him, the Major glided imperceptibly into the shadowy canvas folds of the Big Top to witness their conversation. Both were probably in their fifties, with bodies that had once been gym-toned but were giving way to fat. One was slightly slimmer, the other bulky with every exposed body part, up to and including his neck, covered with a logic-defying assemblage of tattoos.

'Why're the bloody police sniffing round everything?' asked the larger man. His accent was truculently Italian.

'Don't know,' said the thinner, in a voice that had its origins somewhere in Central Europe. His English was less certain than his friend's. 'Health and Safety?'

'That's not police business, is it? Health and Safety have their own snoops. Anyway, the cops've been rooting round in my props.'

'And mine.'

'Yours are bloody knives, so that's no surprise, is it?'

'I tried to get Camille to tell me what was going on. She bloody ignored me, as ever.'

'It's probably just some thieving been going on in the neighbourhood. For which we've got blamed. We circus folk are always the first suspects, aren't we?' But the tattooed one didn't sound reassured by his own reassurance.

'Come on! What are you two gossiping about? You should be getting ready for the show!'

The words were spoken in a strong, almost bullying,

female voice, thick and Slavic. Major Bricket peered briefly round the corner of his canvas hideaway, to see the approach of a woman shorter by a head than either of the men. She was dressed in a black leather bikini, black stiletto heels and a lot of fake tan. Her eyelashes looked like an infestation of black moths.

In spite of her diminutive size, both men jumped to obey her. The one without tattoos jumped quicker, maybe suggesting that he was more aware of the need to meet her wishes. Which might possibly cast him in the role of her husband.

Neither man spoke, as they followed the woman to the Big Top's back entrance. Major Bricket eased himself out of concealment.

The Lavoisier's Circus's programme was lavishly produced and clearly destined to be sold at all the venues on their tour. On the front page was a small rectangle into which a rubber stamp had printed, slightly off-centre, the words 'Ratchetts Common, Stunston Peveril' and the relevant dates.

Major Bricket flipped through the list of acts, hoping to identify the three people on whom he had just been eavesdropping. He didn't have far to look. Although the images had been Photoshopped for maximum glamour, the smaller man and the woman were clearly 'Piotr and Petra – Facing Death Daily from the Razor-Sharp Knives!' Their act was scheduled in the show's first half.

There was a picture of Petra, wearing the black leather bikini and strapped by leather restraints to a moving wheel, with huge knives sticking out, impossibly close to her body. Opposite her stood Piotr, also in black and blindfolded, having just thrown a knife, whose mid-air trajectory seemed destined for his partner's heart.

The tattooed man was billed to appear, after the interval, as 'Massive Mazzini – the Strongest Man on Earth!' A scatter of images showed him bending iron bars, lifting cars, and dangling an adult woman in a bikini from each of his flexed muscular arms.

A recorded fanfare sounded. The lights inside the Big Top went down. Into a spotlight, magnificently dressed in top hat and expensively designed red tailcoat, cut away to reveal a very fine pair of legs, appeared the ring mistress. This must be Bernard's daughter, Camille Lavoisier. She flicked her long whip, which made a very satisfactory crack.

Major Bricket settled back to enjoy the show.

As he had said, it was a very long time since he had been to a circus, and he was surprised at how familiar he found the Lavoisier version of the entertainment. Familiar from his childhood, not from his most recent exposure to the genre.

The last circus he'd actually seen had been struggling against new politically correct prohibitions. No animals had been in evidence, for fear of cruelty having taken place in their training. The clowns had worn no make-up, to avoid the risk of whiteface being seen as some kind of reverse cultural appropriation. And the female trapeze artistes had worn trousers rather than fishnet tights, so that no one could be accused of objectifying women.

The result had been a very watered-down experience, featuring various forms of limp acrobatics and not much else. Cirque du Soleil had a lot to answer for.

The circuses Major Bricket remembered from his childhood, on the other hand, had been rumbustious affairs with lions being tamed, horses jumping through flaming hoops and enough fishnetted female flesh to feed a young man's fantasies for months.

And it was to that vanished style that Lavoisier's Circus harked back. No, there were no big cats, but there was a man who did an act with snakes, which he kept producing from locked boxes. The trapeze artistes' costumes were skimpy enough to titillate young men (or at least the few young men who weren't already sufficiently titillated by online porn).

And the clowns, who had a car off which bits kept falling, along with lots of farting klaxons, were made up in whiteface. Before their act, as was traditional, plastic sheets were laid down to protect the ring from the gunge they would pour over each other. It goes without saying that they were as unfunny as clowns have always been.

For obvious reasons, Major Bricket paid particular attention to the clowns' act. Though he didn't believe that the corpse found at Highfield House had been an actual clown from Lavoisier's Circus, he still watched out for any signs of under-rehearsal in their antics with the collapsible car. Maybe they'd needed to draft in a replacement at short notice, because one of the regulars was missing ...? But no, the clowns' antics were flawlessly performed. And still resolutely unfunny.

The act that did impress him was Piotr and Petra. 'Facing Death Daily from the Razor-Sharp Knives!' was what the programme offered, and that was very much what the audience got. Though he had seen many circus performers over the years and knew about the decades of practice that went into perfecting their tricks, Major Bricket had rarely seen such skill. The jeopardy they were in as they casually tossed knives back and forth looked very real.

And there were one or two variations in the act that he hadn't seen before. Petra, standing with her hand resting on one of the Big Top's giant tentpoles, complained that one of her long painted fingernails needed trimming. And Piotr hurled a knife across the width of the circus ring to snip off the offending part.

The climax towards which the act built was, of course, the one featured in the programme illustration. Petra was strapped by leather thongs to the wheel, which was spun with increasing velocity by her partner, who Major Bricket by now felt sure was her husband. Piotr then checked with an audience member that she couldn't see through the blindfold before he put it on.

Unsighted, he crossed the sawdust and started flinging deadly knives at his wife spinning on the wheel. He had a set of twelve. Before the actual throwing started, Petra, from her position on the wheel, had asked an audience member to pick one of the knives to test on her Lavoisier's Circus programme. The blade sliced through the layers of paper with the speed of a guillotine. Petra assured the audience member that the management would give her a new programme.

What was interesting, to the Major, was the fact that Petra did all the talking. Maybe it was because she had the stronger command of English, but Piotr didn't say a word. And the tone of her talk was almost derisory. She kept challenging him to hit her with one of the knives, complaining when he missed, and commenting on his lack of manliness.

This badinage undoubtedly went over the heads of the children in the Big Top, but for the adults it added an uneasy sexiness to the act.

As her jeopardy increased, so did the intensity of Petra's diminishing of her husband. Once he started throwing the knives, she shouted, 'Come on, Piotr! Show them what a rubbish knife-thrower you are! Cut me to shreds!'

Her goading made the act's high point, when he had slammed every knife into the wheel without spilling a drop of blood, all the more powerful.

Some elements of the trickery Major Bricket had seen before. Piotr had offered his blindfold to an audience member to prove they couldn't see through it. The Major watched assiduously as the knife-thrower took the blindfold and twisted it in his hands, so that, when he put it on, he would be looking through the perforated side. In the course of his travels, Major Bricket had encountered many versions of that trick.

But what intrigued him was that the quality of Piotr and Petra's performance was much higher than that shown in any of the other acts. He wondered why that might be.

Had a double act of their undoubtedly superior skills a special reason for being part of Lavoisier's Circus?

He was also highly impressed by the skills of the ring mistress. Her father may have complained, but, given the state he'd been in in the Goat & Compasses that morning, the Major could not have seen him doing the job as well as his daughter did that afternoon.

Camille Lavoisier was a professional. She had a strong voice and natural stage manner. She made the whole circus company feel like a family and commanded an instant rapport with her audience. For the children, she was a mischievous co-conspirator, for the women she was a complicit companion, and for the men she was subtly sexy without ever losing her dignity. Her allure was increased by the throaty French accent in which she delivered her introductions and comments. If Bernard's daughter was as good at commercial management as she was at presentation, Lavoisier's Circus was in good hands.

There was one surprise, though, after an interval during which the children had feasted on ice cream and candy floss – a change in the scheduled programme. There was no strongman act. 'Massive Mazzini' did not appear.

Instinctively, Major Bricket didn't follow the main crowd leaving the Big Top after the show. He was drawn, once again, round to the back.

There he found, still in her ring-mistress finery, Camille Lavoisier in dispute with someone he recognised. Detective Inspector Pritchett.

'Look,' she was saying passionately, her stage French accent abandoned, 'I am running a business here. Work like mine is already difficult enough without having over-zealous policemen arresting my staff.'

'Are you accusing me of being "over-zealous", Miss Lavoisier?' came the stolid response.

'Yes, Inspector. I am.'

'Thank you. I take that as a compliment.'

'What?'

'The police are constantly being accused in the media of a lack of dedication, of not investigating deeply enough, so to be accused of zealotry is very definitely a compliment.'

Major Bricket once again had the thought that Detective Inspector Pritchett's intellect might be sharper than his manner suggested. The Major had not, incidentally, made any attempt to hide himself on this occasion. Because he already knew Pritchett, there was nothing untoward about approaching him. The Inspector acknowledged his presence with a curt nod.

But he was still dealing with an angry ring mistress. 'I would like to pick you up on another point, Miss Lavoisier,' he said. 'You accused me of "arresting" your staff. Mr Mazzini has not been arrested. He is merely "helping us in our inquiries".'

'But he's not doing that here, is he?' Camille Lavoisier was still enraged. 'He's been taken off to your police station.'

'Merely a matter of convenience, Miss Lavoisier.'

'It may be convenient for you, but it's bloody inconvenient for me! This afternoon's audience didn't get to see a strongman act that they were promised in their programmes. We've got another show this evening. Are you able to tell me whether Massive Mazzini will have finished "helping you with your inquiries" in time to do that performance?'

'No, Miss Lavoisier, I am unable to tell you that. It is frequently difficult to predict the progress of a police inquiry.'

'Oh, I give up!' The ring mistress looked as though she would have liked to crack her whip at the policeman. But she thought better of the idea and just stumped off.

Detective Inspector Pritchett turned a beaming smile

on Major Bricket. 'I am glad to be able to tell you, sir,' he said, 'that you can have the use of your garage and garden back again.'

'Oh?'

'Yes. Our investigations at Highfield House have come to an end.' The Inspector looked at his watch. 'By the time you get back there, the team should have tidied everything up.'

'Well, that's good news.'

'It is indeed, Major. Sometimes, you know, police work can be very simple.'

'Unlike the people who do it.'

Detective Inspector Pritchett took a moment to work out that he had been complimented and then beamed with pleasure.

'Am I to understand, Inspector, that you have solved the case?'

'Ah, now I didn't say that, did I?' came the roguish response.

'Not in so many words, no. But it doesn't take a huge leap of imagination to make a connection between the ending of your investigations at the scene of the crime and the fact that Massive Mazzini is helping you with your inquiries.'

'Not a leap of imagination, Major, but quite possibly a leap to a conclusion.'

'So, you are saying that you have not yet solved the crime?'

'That,' said the detective as he took his leave, 'is exactly what I'm saying.'

But the jaunty manner in which he walked away from the Big Top told the opposite story.

If the Inspector really thought Massive Mazzini was the murderer, Major Bricket found himself unable to agree. He decided that, the Boys in Blue having done their best, he needed to conduct further, private, investigations.

4

The Ring Mistress

'Are you police too?'

Major Bricket's intention to go straight back to Highfield House was halted by the question from Camille Lavoisier. He turned to face her. She had quickly changed out of her ring mistress finery and was wearing the kind of simple white shirt and pale blue jeans that signify considerable expense.

'I'm sorry?'

'I was asking if you were a member of the police force. You seemed to know the Detective Inspector well.'

'I only met him yesterday. Not a voluntary encounter on my part, I can assure you. But he had to act, because it was in my garage that the clown's corpse was found.'

'Ah. You must be the owner of Highfield House. Major . . .?'

'Bricket.'

'Major Bricket – right.'

'And, to spell out my answer to your question – no, I have nothing to do with the police, and my relationship with them has so far been restricted to asking for directions. A state of affairs that I would recommend to anyone.'

'Couldn't agree more.' She nodded thoughtfully. 'Major Bricket, might you have a few moments free to talk about recent events? By that I mean, it goes without saying, the corpse found in your garage.'

Life, the Major often found, was full of serendipities. He had been wondering how to engineer a conversation with Camille Lavoisier on that very subject. And now she had saved him the trouble.

Circus caravans had changed markedly from the cylindrical wooden ones featured in the Enid Blyton books Major Bricket had grown up with. If he hadn't seen the wheels from outside, he wouldn't have known that Camille Lavoisier's home was in any way mobile. From the interior design, he could have been in an upmarket New York apartment.

The caravan comprised, at one end, sitting room, office and kitchen. Behind the doors that led to the other half presumably lay bedroom and bathroom. The décor was mostly glass and metal, modern and minimal. The absence of photographs or family impedimenta suggested that Camille Lavoisier did not share her space with anyone else.

Her manner suggested she didn't gladly share her time with fools, either. Major Bricket felt honoured that she appeared to treat him as an intellectual equal.

Camille seemed relieved to have had her offer of coffee or tea turned down. She wanted to get onto the serious business of their conversation and began, with what the Major suspected was characteristic directness, by saying, 'Since we both, whether we like it or not, seem to have some connection with the murder that's just taken place, I thought it would make sense if we were to pool the information each of us has, with a view to finding out the truth of what happened.' Her manner of speaking was formal, perhaps to emphasise her managerial position.

The Major endorsed her view. 'Excellent idea.'

'Obviously, when I say "information", I use the word to include anything that may have been said to either of us, in confidence, by the police.'

'That goes without saying. Well, I'm afraid, Camille . . . I may call you Camille?'

'Please.'

'The police have told me very little, which is not unusual when they're conducting an investigation. Of course, I've been questioned by Detective Inspector Pritchett. I couldn't give him much relevant intelligence, however, because I only yesterday returned from foreign parts. Croatia. Features some wonderful church architecture, you know.'

'I'll take your word for it. I haven't been there,' she said crisply, unwilling to be sidetracked.

'Inspector Pritchett,' the Major went on, 'in the manner of all policemen, was very cagey about telling me anything related to the case. So, I am somewhat in the dark.'

'Me too. I'm desperate for an explanation of what he's just done with Massimo.'

'"Massimo" being the first name of "Massive Mazzini"?'

'Yes. Why did the Inspector arrest him?'

'To be technical,' the Major pointed out, 'Detective Inspector Pritchett has not arrested Massive Mazzini. He has merely requested the strongman should "help the police with their inquiries".'

Camille Lavoisier snorted derisively. 'Yes, but we all know what that means, don't we?'

The Major's bland 'Not necessarily' was rewarded by another snort. 'I need to know when he'll be free to appear in my circus again. I'm trying to run a business here.'

'Hm.' The Major was silent for a moment. 'And the possibility hasn't occurred to you that Massive Mazzini might be in some way involved in the murder?'

'No way. Massimo may look like a muscle-bound thug, but he's the gentlest creature on God's earth. He wouldn't hurt a fly. Literally. He's a Buddhist.'

Major Bricket expressed no surprise. This was not just because he had been trained to keep a poker face at all times, but also because he had enough experience of life to be unfazed by any quirk of human behaviour. And he'd come across many worse quirks than Buddhism.

He also had enough experience to be unfazed by being alone in the company of a highly attractive woman. His softer emotions – though undoubtedly a part of his psyche – were held in the same check as his more violent ones. He appreciated female beauty and had on occasion enjoyed its benefits. But he recognised the attendant risks. Major Bricket was capable of love, but he was far too canny ever to be caught in a honeytrap.

'Of course,' he said, 'the one rather important detail that prevents me from having useful theories about the murder is that I have no idea of the victim's identity.'

'There I can help you,' said the ring mistress.

'You know who it is?'

'Yes.'

'So – someone who works at the circus?'

'In a way.'

'What does that mean?'

'My father and I have differing views on many aspects of running this enterprise. And we disagree significantly on the matter of staffing.'

'Oh?'

'When I grew up with the circus, it was a tight-knit family business . . . or perhaps I should say it was a tight-knit business of families. Not just the Lavoisiers; a lot of the acts were partners or children of other circus people.

'And, you know, Dad could be great fun back then. Always ready with a joke. Like most of the Lavoisiers, he started out as a performer. Used to do a kind of clown act with a mate of his called Hubert. Not whiteface stuff; they did more, like, comedy sketches.

'There was a famous one called "The Plastered Plasterers", like the classic decorating scene in a pantomime, plastic sheeting laid down on the ring for the mess, the whole business.' She could not curb the enthusiasm in her description. 'Dad and Hubert, who were quite young then, pretended to be very old men – very pissed old men – who'd been given the job of painting a room. Everything that could go wrong did go wrong . . . you know, tripping over ladders, buckets of whitewash spilling everywhere . . .

'I know about it from other people in the circus. He and Hubert did the act long before I was born. Apparently, it always brought the house down. But then Hubert moved on to do other stuff, some kind of animal act, and Dad gave up the performing in favour of management.

'I think a bit of him always wanted to go back to performing. He loved making an audience laugh and found it a lot simpler than controlling a bunch of bolshie circus acts. But he was still always ready with a joke, you know, when I was growing up. Not a great businessman, but a very gentle human being.

'He became increasingly stressed, though, as the financial situation with the circus got worse. But he was still very much a team player. There's a community feeling when you're touring, spending so much time in each other's company – a solidarity, if you like. And my mother was, kind of, the linchpin that held the whole circus family together. Dad relied on her totally. Since she died . . .'

'How long ago was that?'

'Getting on for three years now.'

'I'm sorry.'

'So am I.' Camille's words were heartfelt. 'Anyway, from that time, my father, kind of, went off the rails. I mean, I know he was devastated by his loss, everyone in the circus was . . . but he just fell apart.'

'Is that when the drinking started?' the Major asked.

'It'd always been there in the background, but after Mum's death, it very much moved centre stage. That's why I had to take over the running of the thing. My Dad was no longer . . . what's that horrible expression politicians keep using? "Fit for purpose", that's it.'

'You were talking about disagreements with your father over staffing,' the Major nudged.

'Oh yes. It was partly just the passage of time. The older generation of Lavoisier's performers were dying off, and a lot of their children took the wise decision not to follow them into the circus profession, so staff numbers were down. And then Dad suddenly gave notice to a lot of the older backstage support, leaving a skeleton staff, and booking in local temporary workers in each of the venues we toured to.

'He said it made economic sense, but I don't believe that. It certainly didn't make sense from the point of view of humanity. All those Lavoisier's Circus lifers suddenly out on their ears. It was unlike my Dad. He'd had his failings – the booze being one of them, and an anything-for-the-easy-life laziness another – but he'd always been a caring boss, would do anything to help a staff member out in a personal or financial crisis.'

Camille Lavoisier, the ultimate hard-nosed businesswoman, seemed to be on the verge of tears. Major Bricket intervened, asking, 'And what do you think made him change? Reaction to your mother's death?'

'That was certainly part of it. But not enough to make him turn on his long-term staff. That went against everything he'd ever believed in. I think Dad must've been under pressure in some way.'

'From whom?'

'That's what I don't know. Mum's death couldn't have come at a worse time. Not just emotionally, but for the business. Obviously, we'd suffered badly during Covid. Money was simply running out. Dad was desperately contacting potential sources of finance. We needed to borrow a lot. And he was really an innocent in that kind of world.'

'Do you know whether he did actually borrow any money?'

'He must've done. I know the abysmal financial state Lavoisier's Circus was in at the end of all the lockdowns. The fact that we still exist means Dad must've got funding from somewhere.'

'Your tone of voice, Camille, suggests that he hasn't shared the source of that funding with you.'

'Exactly! God knows how many times I've asked him about it. I've tried everything – catching him off guard when he's drunk. Nothing works. He clams up every time.'

'But, presumably, now you've taken over running the show, you have access to all the bank details?'

'Yes, of course I do. I've been through everything. I can tell you the income and outgoings of Lavoisier's Circus to the last digit. And the sources of all that income ... except for one regular payment.'

'Oh?'

'Ten grand a month.'

The Major let out a low whistle. 'Substantial.'

'And how! I'm afraid it's what's keeping the business afloat. Without it we'd be toast.'

'And no indication of where it's come from?'

'Just an account number.'

'Surely the police could trace that? If there's evidence of criminal activity?'

Camille Lavoisier grimaced. 'Evidence of *what* criminal activity? There is none. Just my suspicion that my father may have got involved with some shady characters for his funding.'

'Hmm.'

'Also ...' For a moment she was uncertain as to whether to continue. She made up her mind. 'Also, for someone of my background, someone who grew up around circus people ... many of whom are of Roma extraction ... going to the police about anything is very definitely off the menu. Sorry, I'm talking about generations of suspicion here.'

'I'm sure you are.'

'Hard habits of mind to break.'

'I can believe that. Of course,' the Major observed, 'you've ended up getting involved with the police anyway. Courtesy of the corpse found in my garage.'

'Yes.'

He tapped his chin thoughtfully. 'Detective Inspector Pritchett must've got something, some solid evidence, to make him suspicious of Massive Mazzini. Any idea what that might be?'

'The only thing I can think of is the iron bar with which the victim was strangled. That really points the finger at him. Massimo's got a lot of props like that. And if it is one of his, there'll be his fingerprints all over it.'

'Yes. You do know, don't you, Camille, that it wasn't strangling by an iron bar that killed the murder victim?'

That had her intrigued. She listened, rapt, as the Major told her about the bullet to the back of the head.

'Traditional gangland execution,' she said.

He did not pass comment on how she came to know that. Instead, he asked, 'No question that the iron bar did belong to Massive Mazzini?'

'Well, I suppose there may be other people in Stunston Peveril who have a collection of iron bars, but he's the obvious one, isn't he?'

'Yes.' He smiled at her irony.

'Obvious enough to raise the suspicions of a baffled British Bobby, anyway.'

Major Bricket didn't share with her his suspicion that there was rather more to Detective Inspector Pritchett than met the eye. 'I couldn't help observing,' he said, 'that the iron bar in question was a fake. It looked like an iron bar, but it had the flexibility of a pipe cleaner.'

Camille Lavoisier smiled a little sheepishly. 'Massimo does use certain tricks in his act. Including the old one of getting a member of the audience to come up and test the validity of an iron bar and then substituting a prop one before he bends it round a tent pole.'

'I suspected something of the sort.' Major Bricket had witnessed the acts of fake magicians from Delhi to Dunedin. No amount of trickery would pull the wool over his eyes.

'But,' Camille hastened to reassure him, 'most of the things Massimo does in his act are completely genuine. It's only for that one trick that he uses the fake iron bar.' It was instinctive for her to assert her performer's integrity.

It was equally instinctive for the Major not to question her assertion. He moved the conversation on, 'When we began talking, you said you knew the identity of the murder victim. Then we got rather sidetracked into your father's business affairs.'

'Yes, I'm sorry.'

'Don't be. It was all useful background stuff. But now, perhaps, you can tell me who the unfortunate young man was.'

'His name is – was – Danny Linton.'

'And can I extrapolate, from what you were saying, that Danny Linton is one of the temporary staff, just taken on for the Stunston Peveril part of the tour?'

'Exactly.'

'So, did you know him well?'

'Hardly at all. Petra – she is the wife of Piotr, the knife-thrower – she acts as kind of company manager and arranges the rotas for the backstage crews. She perhaps knew him better than I did.'

'Does she recruit the temporary workers at each of the venues?'

'No.'

'So, who does?'

'That's another thing I wish I knew. My father produces a list of names and contacts a couple of weeks before we arrive at each stop. The new workers have all been contacted and given instructions. They arrive at the right time and check in with Petra. Then they do what they're told.'

'Are they good workers?'

Camille Lavoisier shrugged. 'Most of them are competent. They can perform rudimentary tasks backstage. And they're no trouble. I haven't had to haul any of them over the coals for laziness or bad timekeeping. Mind you, I wouldn't back any of them to show initiative in an emergency. And it's not like it was in the old days, when everyone had done everything so many times that the circus ran itself.'

'But it must be cheaper than having a large permanent staff?'

Another shrug. 'I guess so. That must be why Dad insists on doing it.'

'Presumably you've asked him where he gets the list of names from?'

'Oh yes. I've asked and asked. But it's the same as with the source of the money that's keeping the show on the road. He won't tell me.'

'So, it's possible that using temporary staff is one of the conditions on which he was granted the funding?'

'Believe me, I've thought through all variations of that possibility, raised it on many occasions – and still can't get anything out of him on the subject.'

Major Bricket nodded thoughtfully. 'You say Danny Linton was local. Do you know any more about him?'

'Not a thing.'

'Petra must have an address for him in her employment records.'

A wry smile. 'I wouldn't count on it. Dad deals with the contracts for the temporary workers.'

'I see.'

The Major left the caravan shortly after, with assurances on both sides that they'd keep each other up to date with any progress they made on their investigation. The ring mistress, having heard nothing further from the police, almost certainly faced the prospect of another performance by Lavoisier's Circus without a strongman.

Major Bricket felt he had made some useful progress. He had the enormous bonus now of a name for the victim. And, given that the boy was a local, there must be someone in Stunston Peveril who could provide information about Danny Linton.

In spite of Detective Inspector Pritchett's assurances, the Major's past dealings with the police had not made him optimistic about the chances of their investigation at Highfield House being all tidied up by the time he got back. It was, after all, hardly twenty-four hours since the discovery of the corpse.

He was pleasantly surprised, though. No sign of any police vehicles parked outside, no Scene of Crime tents or coloured incident tape. They had swept away all traces of their recent presence and even raked the flower beds they had trodden over. Major Bricket was impressed.

He was also pleased that he could now do what he

would have done on first arriving the previous day, had he not been diverted by the appearance of a clown's corpse.

He reached into his pocket for the keys. He didn't have one for the garden shed. If that were locked, it would only raise suspicions. People might wonder whether there was something in there he wanted to hide. And, about any aspect of his life, it had always been a matter of principle to limit the amount of wondering people did.

Inside, the space looked like any other garden shed. In other words, untidy. Spades, forks and hoes leant drunkenly against the walls. The workbench surface was scattered with trowels caked in dried mud, husks of seed pods and cracked plastic flowerpots. The wooden boards of the floor were similarly cluttered. Though Rod Enright had, in theory, been left in charge of garden maintenance, he had been expressly discouraged from tidying the shed.

As he entered, Major Bricket felt the familiar excitement. The development had been completed some decade before and he still felt good about the way its construction had been kept from the suspicious eyes of Stunston Peveril.

Obviously, he had had the right contacts, used to dealing with unusual security projects. They had arrived at Highfield House in vans, suitably disguised as landscape gardening contractors, and did most of the work while the Major was abroad on another assignment. To the denizens of Stunston Peveril, having landscape gardening done was an entirely acceptable – even admirable – use of one's resources, which could only serve to raise the tone of the village. They watched with approval as large amounts of soil were loaded onto trucks in front of the house and then driven away. Because of the geography of the plot, and its high hedges, they couldn't see what was actually being done in the back garden. Which was perhaps just as well.

That afternoon, gleefully, the Major found the relevant wooden strut supporting the shed's interior wall. It looked just like all the others, discoloured and grubby. Until, that is, he turned it to one side to reveal a metal control panel, centred on a keyhole. The relevant key already in his hand, he slotted it in and clicked sideways. Then he entered a remembered code into the keypad and stood back to witness something which he never found less than pleasurable.

There was an uncanny silence as a gap appeared between the floor's central boards. This widened as they drew further apart and some noiseless vacuum system ate up the surface dust and clutter, preventing it from falling into the void.

The lights below had been triggered by the turning of the key and revealed a gleaming metal staircase about six feet across. As soon as the floorboards on either side stopped moving, Major Bricket walked down into his secret sanctum.

Although it was some months since he had last been there, by some technological wizardry everything was gleaming clean – the shiny metal of the walls, the dark wood of the many cupboards and lockers that stood against them. At one end of the space, there was a desk with a sophisticated array of controls facing eight screens, which had been automatically switched on at the same time as the lights. All but one showed live footage from the seven continents.

But the computer stuff could wait. Major Bricket had other priorities. He found the right key and opened a tall metal cupboard riveted to the side wall of his underground domain. Opening the doors revealed serried ranks of guns – rifles upright in slots on the lower level, handguns attached to metal pegs above them. Each weapon was locked in place by a metal cable with a numerical padlock.

He looked appreciatively at the racks of weaponry, before selecting an old favourite, a Smith & Wesson Model 14 .38 Special. Also known as the Target Masterpiece, the revolver had a six-inch barrel and used to be issued to LAPD officers in the 1970s. Major Bricket, instinctively remembering the code, released it from its cable. He found the Smith & Wesson the best of his guns for target practice, and enjoyed the natural weight of it in his hand.

With the relevant key, he opened the ammunition drawer and slotted six bullets into the chamber. From another drawer he produced and put on a pair of noise-cancelling ear defenders. He then pressed a button on the control desk and metal doors at the opposite end of the room concertinaed back to reveal a row of targets. They were cardboard torsos with heads, unmarked by bullet holes. Generally grey in colour, there were dark charcoal circles where the heart and the forehead would be.

At the other end of the gallery, behind the chair facing his control desk, there was a silver-coloured line on the floor. Major Bricket stood behind it and raised the revolver to optimum firing position.

Though firearms did not feature in his retirement plans, there were still certain skills that he wished to keep up to standard, so he fired two rounds of six bullets at the targets in his shooting range. The first six pierced the middles of the charcoal heart rings on the torsos. After he'd reloaded, the second six went higher, producing perfectly centred holes in the cardboard foreheads.

Reload again, and the Major pressed another button on the console. At the end of the gallery, the punctured targets peeled off automatically, to be replaced by new ones. Another button press, and the targets started to move horizontally. They were on some kind of loop, six visible at any given moment, with the rest out of sight behind the back wall.

He turned a dial to increase their speed. Then he once again stood behind the silver line and raised the revolver.

A moment to adjust to the speed of the passing targets, then the Major fired six shots in rapid succession. When they came back into sight, six more foreheads had bullet holes in them.

As he started to reload, Major Bricket was aware of a change in the lighting. Damn, in his keenness to start shooting, he had omitted to reclose the floor above him.

He looked up to see the outline of a human figure at the top of the stairs.

5

Dinner at Highfield House

'I never knew you had this down here.'

Although they hadn't met for some time and the speaker was just an outline against the daylight, Major Bricket recognised the voice. It was Rod Enright, the boy whose dying mother Sylvia he had promised he would keep an eye on. The boy who was supposed to have been looking after the Highfield House garden. And who hadn't made a very good job of it.

The Major berated himself for lack of basic tradecraft in leaving the entrance to his cellar open. But the damage was done. There was no point in putting pressure on Rod to forget what he had seen. Major Bricket's considerable experience in such situations had taught him that bullying people to keep schtum never worked. Collaboration was always a much more effective approach than coercion.

'No, that's the idea,' he responded to the boy's words, 'that nobody knows it's down here.' The Major made a gesture of welcome to the space. 'Come and have a look round, Rod.'

The boy came cautiously down the steps, again murmuring in amazement, 'I never knew this place existed.'

'Well, that was, kind of, the point,' said the Major.

'To keep it away from prying eyes. And I think it's the moment to rule out the possibility of more prying eyes appearing.'

He pressed some buttons on the control panel and, silently and seamlessly, the floorboards above them closed together, to Rod's awestruck amazement.

'But what do you do down here?' the boy asked.

Only briefly did the Major consider the option of some fluffy talk of hobbies. Rod may have been only eighteen, but he wasn't stupid. He'd seen the revolver, he'd seen the targets, he'd seen the open gun cupboard. There was no point in telling him anything but the truth.

'As you will have worked out,' said the Major, 'I do shooting practice down here. And' – he gestured to the computer equipment – 'a lot of administrative work.'

Rod didn't ask what he might be administering. If a plan that was shaping in the Major's head came to fruition, he'd have plenty of time to find that out.

The looks that the new arrival was casting on the gun cupboard revealed a fascination with weapons which has long been common to all eighteen-year-olds. 'Quite a selection you've got here, Major.'

'Yes,' their owner agreed. Again, he made no attempt to explain away the presence of a private armoury in Stunston Peveril. Instead, he gestured to the revolver in his hand. 'Have you ever fired one of these, Rod?'

The boy shook his head, unashamedly intrigued by the idea.

'Would you like to have a go?'

Rod couldn't believe what he was being offered. 'Would I? And how!'

Major Bricket used the relevant controls to stop the

targets moving and handed across the loaded revolver. 'Have you used a handgun before?'

The boy shook his head. 'No. But I've seen plenty fired in movies.'

The Major did not think it appropriate to mention that the level of accuracy demonstrated in gunfights on film was astronomically higher than that ever witnessed in real life. But he approved of the stance Rod took behind the silver line. He'd learnt something from watching those movies.

'Aim for the hearts,' said the Major. 'Fire in your own time,'

Six shots in rapid succession. Six targets with bullet holes in the circles of their hearts. Rod hadn't wasted his time when watching those movies.

'That was remarkable. Have you really never used a handgun before?'

'Never.'

The Major nodded as he took the information in. Then he said, 'I think your talents, Rod, are wasted by being a gardener.'

That prompted a sheepish grin.

'Come to dinner at the house this evening,' the Major went on. 'Seven o'clock. Wear a jacket and tie.'

Major Bricket had always had standards.

'I knew letting that riffraff onto Ratchetts Common was a bad idea,' said Viscount Wintle. His grumpiness was tempered by a certain satisfaction at having had his gloomy prognostications proved right. 'Didn't I say that to you, Perpetua?'

'Yes, Gerald,' his wife admitted patiently. 'Many times.'

The Viscount turned for more validation to the third person drinking coffee in the Yellow Morning Room. 'You've heard me say it too, haven't you, Piers?'

The Australian, of course no longer dressed as a kangaroo, had stayed overnight after the costume ball. He, needless to say, had a stately home of his own, Highhouse Hall, a mere fifteen miles away, but the idea of spending a night at Fincham Abbey amused him. The whole estate was so tacky and ill-maintained. The Wintles did not have enough servants. They had had to recruit people from the village to put on the ball. The permanent staff they did have looked worn-down and harassed.

And, among that permanent staff, there wasn't a butler. How shaming. One of the first things Lord Piers Goodruff had done when he bought Highhouse Hall had been to buy the most expensive butler on the market. The man's previous employers, in different parts of the world, had all been at the top echelons of society, captains of industry, internet moguls, Hollywood stars. He had worked in America, Australia and the Gulf States, so he probably knew as much about international affairs as his new master. If not more. Not that anyone would have known it. True to the traditions of his calling, the butler never volunteered an unsolicited opinion on anything. What went on behind his impassively correct features was unfathomable. But he ran everything in his employer's world with immaculate efficiency.

The man, who gloried in the name of Murkish, was one of the noble peer's proudest possessions. (Goodruff regarded all of his staff, along with his mistresses, as personal possessions. After all, he'd paid for them.)

Comparing the butlerless Fincham Abbey to his own

immaculately made-over Highhouse Hall gave him a superior glow. And one of the main aims of Lord Piers Goodruff's life was attaining a superior glow. It gave him an enormous charge to know that, in every arena, he was better than other people. Or, at least, richer.

He agreed with his host that 'letting that riffraff onto Ratchetts Common was a bad idea'. He also agreed that the Viscount had made his views on the subject crystal clear. 'Even in the short time I've been here, Greg, I've heard you say it a good few times.'

'I mean,' the Viscount grumbled on, 'to have the police arrive at Fincham Abbey for any other purpose than to ask my permission for them to do something ...' The appalling nature of the event robbed him of words.

'It was perfectly logical for them to do so,' his wife soothed. 'You were known in Stunston Peveril to have a large selection of clown outfits assembled for the costume ball. A murder victim was found wearing a clown outfit. It made sense for the police to ask you if one of your collection was missing ... particularly as it proved to be the case that one was missing.'

Viscount Wintle emitted the kind of 'Harrumph' that can only be emitted by someone whose family has generations of practice in the art of harrumphing. He followed it with the assertion that this was not the kind of murder that 'people of our sort' ought to get involved in.

'I mean, there is a social order to be maintained. Lord Erroll in Kenya in 1941 – that was a perfectly respectable murder. He was an Old Etonian, even though he was kicked out of the place. And he was having an affair with Diana, Lady Broughton, whose husband Jock Delves Broughton was a Baronet. All of them "our sort of people".

I wouldn't mind being caught up in that sort of murder. But the idea the police come to Fincham Abbey to question me about the death of a temporary circus worker...' Again, the outrage was too intense to be put into words.

'Gregory,' Perpetua pointed out, 'the police were only doing their job.'

He didn't think that merited a full 'harrumph'. He merely grunted. 'Well, why do they not regard it as their job to do important things, like arresting hunt saboteurs?'

The Viscountess knew that this could be the opening salvo in what could be a long bombardment on the subject, so she adroitly redirected the conversation towards their guest. 'What is your view, Piers, of the efficiency of the British police?'

'I've had very few dealings with them,' he replied serenely, 'but those I have had have been extremely satisfactory. Incidentally,' he went on, 'you know that guy who was at the Costume Ball dressed as a sheikh...? Major... somebodyorother...?'

'Major Bricket,' Perpetua supplied.

'Yeah. And it was in his garage that the body was found?'

'It was.'

'Has he got any connection with the circus?'

'Not so far as I know,' said the Viscountess. 'But then I know very little about him.'

'You, Greg?'

'Never met the fellow.'

'Yes, you did,' his wife corrected him. 'At the costume ball last night. He was dressed as a sheikh.'

'Oh, I remember. Winchester man.' The way he said the words, it wasn't an unreserved compliment.

'But do you know anything about him?' Lord Goodruff insisted.

'Not a sausage.'

'Hmm.' The peer sounded distracted. 'I'm always wary of people nobody knows anything about.'

Though he played up to the image of the crass Australian, Lord Goodruff was a man of high intelligence, with an intimate familiarity with the more secretive areas of international affairs.

A fickle friend and a dangerous enemy.

'I can assure you,' said Venetia Clothbury to Mollie Greenford in the Gingham Tea Shop, 'that I know all the details about the murder.'

This was not an unusual statement from her. She knew all the details about everything. Her companion mentally prepared supplies of salt (to take pinches of) before the statement began.

'Major Bricket, as I told you, Mollie,' said Venetia Clothbury, 'worked arranging security for the Royal Family's foreign visits. And that is a job which does bring with it certain risks.'

'Oh? How do you know that?'

'I know it because my late husband, Sydney, who knew a great many intimate secrets of the Royal Family, confided in me about the matter. "Venetia," he told me with some frequency, "anyone who works for the Royal Family does immediately open themselves up to a certain level of risk." And Sydney always knew what he was talking about.'

'Ah,' said Mollie Greenford.

'So, the work that Major Bricket used to do was work

in which he made enemies. In dealing with foreign powers, it is always easy to put noses out of joint. And certain ethnic groups never forget having their noses put out of joint. Particularly in the Middle East, potentates do not like to be made to look like clowns. And that's what Major Bricket has clearly done. The body dressed in a clown suit found in his garage is a warning from a foreign potentate. The message to the Major is: "I have not forgotten how, prior to a recent Royal visit, you made me look like a clown. This murder is just a warning. You will be the next victim."'

Venetia Clothbury paused for effect and was a little miffed when Mollie Greenford curtailed her pause. 'But I thought the police had arrested someone from Lavoisier's Circus.'

Venetia's edifice of conjecture was not so easily demolished. 'That's what they want you to think,' she said with a knowing wink. 'The police are obeying orders direct from Buckingham Palace. The official line is that the murderer is someone from the circus. The truth is being suppressed to avoid the danger of an international incident.'

'Are you sure, Venetia? I mean—'

'Of course I'm sure, Mollie. Have you ever known me to be wrong?'

'We-ell . . .' said Mollie Greenford awkwardly.

As he spruced himself up in the bathroom before dinner, the delicious smells emanating from the kitchen took Major Bricket straight back to the streets of Hanoi where he had first met Nga Luong. He recalled the successful job they had worked on out there and the reasons why she could never return to the land of her birth.

He hoped her relocation, which he had arranged, to the Green Lotus Thai Restaurant in Stunston Peveril had proved of benefit to her. Certainly, Nga Luong never complained. But that might have been a national characteristic, or a habit carried over from her previous career. She rarely gave any hint as to what she was actually thinking.

Rod hadn't much experience of foreign food, but he didn't want to look unadventurous, so he took one of the proffered crispy cylinders.

'Dip in the sauce,' said Nga Luong.

Obediently, he poked it into the garlic mayonnaise and took a bite. First, nothing. Then, wow! It was hard to separate his sensations. He was just aware how the crunchy exterior gave way to the softness within. And how that moment coincided with the explosion of tastes in his mouth – fishy, spicy, peppery.

'Wow!' he said. 'That's amazing! What's it called in ... where you come from?' Geography had never been Rod's strong suit at school.

She smiled. 'I think it would be easier if I told you in English. Nearest translation would be "breaded seafood spring rolls".'

'Ah,' said Rod again. He didn't particularly notice what excellent, almost perfect, English Nga spoke. If he'd ever been to the Green Lotus Restaurant, he might have found this odd. When she was at work, her accent was strong. Once again, she was giving the public what they expected from someone Thai ... or, indeed, Vietnamese.

Rod took another delicious bite of his breaded seafood spring roll. If all the starters on the table were as good, he would be in gastronomic heaven. And the Major had provided him with an excellent Belgian beer as well. Bricket himself was drinking whisky. So was Nga Luong. From what they said, Rod got the impression they had often shared bottles when working together in Vietnam. He wondered idly what kind of work they'd been doing there. There was so much he didn't know about them.

He was brought back from his reverie by the Major who, after swirling the ice in his Scotch and taking a sip, revived an earlier strand of conversation. 'Are you saying, Rod, that you actually knew Danny Linton?'

'A bit.' The young man looked uncomfortable, and it wasn't just because of the unaccustomed tie around his neck. He'd been awkward on first arrival at Highfield House, but a few Belgian beers and the sight of Nga Luong's spread had relaxed him. Now, suddenly, he was uptight again.

'Define "a bit".'

'Well, Major, Danny and I were school together.'

'Here at Stunston Peveril?'

'Yes. The village primary. The original plan was that, after playschool, I was going to a private prep school but, after Dad walked out, Mum couldn't afford it. So, I went to Stunston Peveril Church of England Primary.'

'Yes, I knew that.' As often happened, Major Bricket didn't say how he knew.

'Did you continue in state education?' asked Nga Luong. As well as an English accent, she had somehow assimilated a great deal of information about the systems and institutions of her adopted country. (She was, in fact, a human sponge for knowledge. She could never get enough. Every time she encountered a new subject, she wanted to find out all the details. Since her arrival in England, she had gobbled down everything there was to know about, respectively, the development and potential uses of AI, English painting of the seventeenth and eighteenth centuries, and the Metaphysical poetry of John Donne and Abraham Cowley.)

'For a while,' Rod replied to her question. 'The primary and then the comprehensive at Duckton. For the last part of my secondary education, I went to public school. Somehow, Mum had managed to leave money for that. Or maybe it was some kind of bursary? I really don't know the details.'

Major Bricket ate on, impassively.

'And then will you be going on to university?' Nga Luong, as ever, was hungry for facts.

The boy looked uncomfortable again. 'No, I . . . um . . . exams . . . I'm OK at remembering stuff but writing what I remember into essays . . . What I mostly enjoyed at school was playing rugby.'

'What position?' asked the Major.

'Scrum half.'

That got a nod of approval.

'I was never very good at exams,' Rod admitted. 'And university . . . it never worked out.'

'Don't worry,' said the Major. 'Some of the finest minds in the country have never set foot in a university.'

'You wouldn't think that, the way some of the staff at school went on about it.'

'Anyway, you must have been under a lot of stress

these last few years,' continued the Major, 'with your mother dying and—'

'I'd rather not talk about it!'

Gracefully, the Major changed tack. 'Anyway, tell me what you know about Danny Linton.' He never got diverted for long from his main line of enquiry.

'Very little. Yes, we were at the same schools, but he was three or four years older than me, so we never saw much of each other. And I haven't seen him at all since I left Duckton.'

'What kind of a reputation did he have at primary school?'

'Bad. If there was any trouble, Danny Linton would be involved in it somehow.'

'Bad behaviour at the comprehensive, too?' asked the Major.

'I didn't see much of him there. There were rumours of antisocial behaviour from him flying around, but no detail. And I was only at Duckton for a few years. Once I was off at boarding school, I didn't hear anything about what was happening in Stunston Peveril.'

'Do you know what Danny did after he'd left school?'

'Not in much detail, no. I heard that he'd tried lots of different jobs but didn't stick at any of them.'

'And you're sure you hadn't seen him recently? The last week? Since the Lavoisier's Circus has been here? Because apparently Danny Linton was employed by them as a casual worker.'

Rod shook his head. 'Haven't seen him.'

'Do you know where he lived?'

'Heard he'd moved out of the village. Where to, I've no idea.'

Major Bricket nodded, as if fully satisfied with the answers he'd received. But his long experience of getting information out of people told him that Rod Enright was holding something back. What that was would be uncovered in time, but now was not the moment to probe further. The look he exchanged with Nga Luong confirmed that she felt the same.

She went to the kitchen and the starters were replaced, almost imperceptibly, by main courses. For Rod's benefit, Nga identified them. In English. 'That is steamed fish in rice paper, served with rice noodles and lemongrass oil. This one is flaked chicken with water spinach . . .'

The list went on. And when she started detailing all the sauces, Rod felt his brain was close to capacity. There was a certain amount of gratified chomping before the dialogue resumed.

'With regard to the murder,' said the Major, 'I feel there are things we should do.'

'Certainly,' said Nga Luong.

'What kind of things?' asked Rod.

'Well, first, prevent a miscarriage of justice.'

'What, you mean a miscarriage of justice to the strong-man, the one who's been arrested for the crime?'

'I'm not sure, Rod, that he has yet technically been arrested.'

'Really, Major? Everyone in Stunston Peveril says he has been.'

Why wasn't the Major surprised to hear that? He knew that the village bush telegraph worked much faster than any posting on a social media platform.

'He's still being kept for questioning, that's certainly true.'

'Which must mean,' said Nga Luong, 'that the police have got more evidence against him than just his fingerprints on the fake iron bar.'

'I agree, Nga. Particularly since it wasn't the iron bar that killed Danny Linton. So, I'll investigate back at the circus . . .' He cast an intense look in her direction. 'And could you check out the other details . . . in your usual way?'

She nodded, reinforcing Rod's impression, which had been growing as they ate the meal, that there was a lot more to Nga Luong than met the eye. The boy was starting to lose focus a bit, a common by-product of drinking Belgian beer when you're eighteen, but he still had the feeling that he was part of a very special evening.

And that perception was only intensified when Major Bricket announced, 'I'm convinced there's something very serious wrong in Stunston Peveril, of which Danny Linton's murder is only a symptom. I am determined to find out what's actually going on here. And I should mention at this point that there is a time pressure.'

'Why's that?' asked Rod.

'Because Lavoisier's is a touring circus. They're only in Stunston Peveril for a week. That's their pattern – arrive and set up on Sunday, two performances a day Monday until Saturday. Strike everything after the second show on Saturday, then drive through the night to their next venue and start all over again.

'It's already Tuesday. At the moment – excluding that old Golden Age favourite of a homicidal lunatic escaped from a local asylum – we have all the potential suspects gathered here in one place. On Saturday evening, Lavoisier's Circus will be on its way out of

Stunston Peveril. We need to solve this murder before that happens.'

'Of course we do,' said Rod, thrilled by that inclusive 'we'.

'So,' the Major continued, 'the next part of our investigative process will be to find out what evidence Detective Inspector Pritchett has that makes him so sure Massive Mazzini – that's the strongman,' he said for Rod's benefit, 'is the perpetrator. In that and subsequent quests, I hope I can rely on both of you to assist me.'

Nodding, Nga Luong smiled knowingly. She had much experience of working with Major Bricket. The ride was often fraught with danger, but never less than exhilarating.

As Rod Enright gave his assent, he felt sheer delight. To be included in the Major's plans for an investigation was more than he could ever have wished for.

Though he wasn't aware how much of the Major's plans might include investigating him.

6

Cast-Iron Evidence

'You could leave them here,' said the Major.

Nga Luong looked at the pots and pans piled high on the kitchen table, along with the water spinach cutter, the crinkle-edged knife and the bottles containing all her sauces. Then she looked at him for explanation.

'Presumably, you have other sets of kitchenware at the restaurant?'

'Of course I do.'

'Well then, leave these here for the next time you cook for me.'

She nodded and started to find cupboard space for her equipment. It was not in her nature to express her feelings out loud, but her body language showed satisfaction with the suggestion he had just made.

The Major stood by the door, swirling in his glass what would possibly be the day's last whisky. 'Bright boy, isn't he?'

'Rod?'

'Yes.'

Nga Luong nodded thoughtfully. 'He's come through difficult times,' she observed.

'Yes. Nearly went to the bad, I've heard. Well, did go

to the bad after his mother died. Got into the wrong company. Learnt how to be a thief. I only found out about it later. At the time it was happening, I was on an assignment in Nigeria, which took a lot longer than anticipated.'

'I heard about that,' said Nga Luong.

The Major didn't linger in memories. He moved on. 'Rod has skills. Not academic skills; ones that will prove of much more benefit to him in the real world.'

'And those few years of boarding school can't have done him any harm.'

'I hope not. Certainly kept him out of trouble, during term times at least.'

'Strange ...' Nga reflected, 'how they were so poor when his mother was bringing him up as a single parent, so he goes to state schools. But, a couple of years after she died, there was money to send him to public school. How did that come about?'

'Some kind of bursary, I believe,' the Major replied, swiftly moving on. 'I was just thinking about the time I spent in Vietnam ...'

'Oh yes?'

'... and the idea of "hungry ghosts". I was surprised how many people I met out there who still believed in them.'

'"Hungry ghosts" have a long history. They came from Chinese Buddhism. The idea is that someone who has been ungenerous in their life or dies an unhappy death or is not properly buried near their home will wander for some time, waiting to be reborn. The hungry ghosts cause mischief and demand offerings of food.'

'And there are mediums who can make contact with the hungry ghosts?' the Major suggested.

'Of course. In Vietnam many people believe that.'

'I was just thinking how convenient such a person would be when it came to a murder inquiry.'

'How so?'

'Obviously. Because the medium could ask the victim about the circumstances of their death.'

'Ah. I see. And are you asking me, Major, whether I have such mediumistic skills and could arrange a quick interview with Danny Linton?'

'It would be awfully convenient if you did.'

Nga Luong turned a sharply focused look on Major Bricket. 'Convenient, yes. But I am afraid I do not have such skills. Nor do I believe that anyone has such skills. Mediums make their livings from the credulity of the ignorant. Any divination I do does not involve hungry ghosts. It involves online research on my laptop.'

The Major smiled a rare smile. He had been sending her up. Nga Luong wished she was better at telling when Major Bricket was joking.

But she had a response ready. In her best sub-Confucian manner, as if delivering one of her fortune cookies in the Green Lotus Restaurant, she said, 'When birds fly above the clouds, they cannot see the ground.'

She was glad that Major Bricket looked pleasingly confused.

But when she got back to her flat above the Green Lotus Restaurant, Nga Luong was certainly not expecting any supernatural help with her researches. She didn't believe in hungry ghosts, or any other kinds of ghosts. Or mediums. Nga Luong had always dealt in the here and now.

But her 'here and now' encompassed a respect for the past. And a particular respect for her deceased mother and father. The honouring of previous generations came naturally to her, as it did to most Vietnamese. In her sitting room, she had a small altar to each parent and that evening she burnt incense in front of both, before she started her night's work.

Nga Luong's skills, apart from cooking and absorbing information like a sponge, concerned computers. Training at school in Vietnam and a couple of American universities had brought her a very high proficiency in the art of finding information online. And if her researches sometimes strayed into illegality and overfamiliarity with the dark web . . . well, that was just a price to be paid. It was also the reason why Major Bricket had had to bail her out of Vietnam. And the reason why she could never re-enter the country of her birth.

Her employment in Vietnam had been under conditions of extreme secrecy. She had been well paid by authorities happy not to ask how she obtained the information they required. So long as she came up with the goods, that was all that mattered to them.

The thought that they might back her up and get her out of a hole if she came unstuck was laughable. Suddenly, her employers would never have heard of her. They would have no record of any work they'd commissioned from her. She had always known the risks involved. Many of her sources were unaware that she was stealing data from them, and if they had found out, their revenge would have been swift and terminal.

What she had been very well paid to do back then was to build up dossiers on people, background histories going a long way into the past. And what she had frequently uncovered were the gobbets that her paymasters were really looking for: evidence of criminality.

With her sudden transplantation to England, she saw no reason to allow her skills to rust. So, she was slowly building up dossiers on all the residents of Stunston Peveril.

'I accompanied Detective Inspector Pritchett and his sidekick when they searched Massimo's caravan.'

The following morning, the Wednesday, they were once again sitting in the luxury of Camille Lavoisier's caravan. Dressed, as before, in the kind of simplicity that costs a lot – this time loose blue shirt and white jeans – she looked stunning. And more than ready to share with Major Bricket any information that might help get her circus team back to its full strength.

'Which is his?' The big picture window looked out over the other caravans.

Camille pointed. 'That one over there's Massimo's.'

The caravan looked old and pretty shabby. Next to it was another of the same vintage, rather better maintained.

'That's my dad's.'

'And the smart one the other side of your dad's?'

'Belongs to Petra and Piotr.'

The caravan was very up to date. Parked next to it was an electric BMW i4 M50.

'Pricey car,' the Major observed. 'Is that theirs?'

'Yes.'

'Circus performance clearly pays more than I'd expected.'

'Sadly, no. Apparently Petra was left some money by a relative in Poland.'

'Ah.' The Major looked thoughtful for a moment. 'Sorry, Camille, I got sidetracked. Why did you go with

Pritchett when he and his sidekick examined Massimo's caravan?'

'I felt,' she replied, 'that, since Massimo was at the police station and unable to show the Inspector round himself, someone should be present to look after his interests.'

'To see that the police didn't plant any evidence?'

'I didn't say that,' was Camille's judicious response. 'But the fact is that families like mine have not, over the years, been given reason to have a high opinion of what are called "the proper authorities".'

'Very gracefully put,' said the Major. 'But I'm assuming you didn't see the unimpeachable Detective Inspector Pritchett – or his sidekick – plant incriminating evidence?'

'I did not.'

'But you did see them *find* some incriminating evidence?'

'I did. Very badly hidden it was, too. Against the wall, behind the fold-up table in Massimo's sitting room ... well, hardly sitting room ... sitting area, I suppose. His caravan is of a fairly primitive design.'

The Major couldn't stop himself from saying, 'Unlike this one?'

She smiled a wry confirmation, then went on, 'Detective Inspector Pritchett and his sidekick found the gun which had killed Danny Linton. Also, an opened jiffy bag containing a thousand pounds in twenties. It was addressed to Massimo.'

'A pretty thorough frame-up,' the Major observed.

'Yes. But a perfect find for a policeman like Detective Inspector Pritchett, in whom – what shall I say – imagination is not a dominant characteristic?'

'Again, very graceful.' The Major chuckled. 'You would have a very promising future in the Diplomatic Service.'

She awarded him a small smile.

'Can I just ask, Camille, what is the level of security round here backstage?'

She shrugged. 'You mean, do people lock their caravans when they go out?'

'That is exactly what I mean.'

'The answer depends very much on the individual ... and is probably a reflection of how much valuable stuff they keep there.' She gestured round her own minimalist elegance. 'I always lock this when I go out because, apart from some valuable personal possessions, this is where I keep the cash takings from the shows – and a surprising number of people in the places where we tour still prefer to use cash.'

'But other circus members might be less punctilious on security?'

'Certainly. Petra and Piotr are very tight on it, but that might be because they don't want anyone to find the props they use to create their illusions.'

Major Bricket nodded. 'And Massimo?'

Camille Lavoisier's lips screwed up wryly. 'Massimo is not great on security. His strongman act is very well organised, but that's about the only thing in his life that is.'

'So, it would be in character for him to have left his caravan unlocked, as an open invitation to anyone who wished to plant incriminating evidence on him?'

'It would be entirely in character,' Camille Lavoisier confirmed.

'And for him to be confused by police interrogation and come across a lot guiltier than he is?'

'That, I'm afraid, would also be entirely in character. And, though he's spent a lot of time in this country, his English is still not good. Any half-decent lawyer could make mincemeat of him.' Camille Lavoisier turned her shrewd grey eyes on the Major. 'Are you going to see Detective Inspector Pritchett, to challenge his reading of the case, and tell him that Massimo didn't do it?'

He shook his head. 'Regretfully, that kind of approach would have no effect on a man like the Inspector. He's set in his ways and he's currently congratulating himself on the superior investigative skills which have enabled him to solve the Lavoisier's Circus murder so tidily and speedily. The only thing that'd make him change his mind would be if I were to go to him with incontrovertible proof that someone else committed the crime.'

'And do you think you can provide that proof?' asked Camille Lavoisier.

'Of course,' said Major Bricket. 'Or at least I can have a damned good try.'

After he left her, the ring mistress watched him thread his way between the other caravans. Her expression did not suggest that she had been reassured by their encounter. If anything, as she reached for the phone, she looked troubled.

He'd felt his mobile vibrate while he was with Camille, so he checked the text as he left Ratchetts Common. It didn't surprise him that Nga Luong was already reporting back with the results of her research. Much of what she listed was confirmation of things he had already suspected. Among what she regarded as new information was the fact that Rod Enright had been fostered by a family whose surname was Root.

Twelve o'clock just having sounded from the Stunston Peveril church clock, Major Bricket felt it was the perfect time for a pint of Devil's Burp in the Goat & Compasses. The good weather continuing, most of the pub's clientele were once again sitting in the garden, but the Major made straight for 'Crocker's Corner' as a likely source of the information he needed.

The personnel hadn't changed from his visit the day before. Crocker Fosbury was in prime position pontificating behind the bar. Brother Derek sat on the other side, as ever agreeing with everything anyone else said. And Bernard Lavoisier continued to mumble disconsolately into his brandy.

The Major was roundly welcomed, particularly by Derek, gladdened perhaps by the arrival of another person to agree with. Major Bricket's offer to buy a round added to his popularity. Like him, the two brothers opted for a pint of Devil's Burp, and the circus owner (if that's what he still was) asked for another large brandy.

A few exchanges about how the Major was finding it being back in Stunston Peveril were quickly dealt with, before they all moved on to what had been the village's obsessive topic of conversation for the last few days.

'I'm convinced,' the landlord announced, 'that they've arrested the wrong man. That strongman never did it.'

Intrigued to hear his own views echoed, the Major asked Crocker how he had reached that conclusion. Would the landlord's thinking coincide with his own?

It didn't take long for the removal of that possibility. 'My current view,' said the sage of Stunston Peveril, 'is that the murder was the work of aliens.'

'I'd go along with you there,' the loyal Derek concurred.

'And do you have any basis for saying that?' came a polite enquiry from the Major.

'Yes, of course. You only have to think about how the victim was dressed.'

'Sorry? What do you mean?'

'The clown suit. That was the giveaway.'

'The giveaway,' Derek echoed.

'The way I see it is . . .' Crocker Fosbury was getting into his stride now '. . . dressing the dead body in a clown suit could only be the action of someone unfamiliar with English "funerary customs".' This expression was clearly something he had read somewhere, and he pronounced the two words with fastidious pride.

'I suppose that's possible,' said the Major dubiously.

'And who could know less about English funerary customs than an alien from another planet?' the landlord concluded.

'Well, quite a lot of people, actually,' said the Major, with perfect logic. 'And, incidentally, where did these aliens come from?'

'Another planet,' Crocker repeated mysteriously.

'Do we know which one?'

'No, they've deliberately kept that information to themselves.'

'Ah. And their spaceship landed in Stunston Peveril?'

'Oh yes.'

'Do you know where in Stunston Peveril?'

'No. They covered their tracks very effectively. They've deliberately not left any trace. But I can assure you,' the landlord announced ponderously, 'that that is what happened.'

'That is what happened,' said Derek, who had been starved of opportunities to agree during his brother's long speech.

'It's obvious!' said Crocker, with the triumphalism of a mathematician who has just solved a theorem which has puzzled his international colleagues for generations.

Major Bricket looked thoughtful, as if seriously considering the claim. Then he asked, 'Have you thought about sharing your theory with the police?'

'Ah, no,' the landlord replied cannily. 'Because that is exactly what they would want me to do.'

'"They" being . . . ?'

'The aliens, of course.' Crocker Fosbury spoke as if to a child who was rather slow of perception. 'You see, if I took what I know to the police, the aliens would immediately know that I was on to them and, for me, the consequences could be dire.'

'You are saying that the police are in league with the aliens?'

'Yes, I am,' said Crocker, 'At least two of the officers at the local station are aliens in disguise.'

'In disguise,' Derek echoed.

The Major took a long, pensive swallow of Devil's Burp. Then he said, 'Well, it's certainly a theory.' Without straying over the boundaries of truth, this could be read by the landlord as a commendation. That was unquestionably how the recipient took it, as he rewarded himself with his own long draught of Devil's Burp.

'Something I wanted to ask you about, Crocker,' said the Major, 'concerns Rod . . . you know, Sylvia Enright's son . . .'

'Oh yes? We were talking about him yesterday.'

'That's right. He drinks in here sometimes, doesn't he?'

An expression of caution crossed the landlord's face. 'Well, the boy occasionally comes in for a lemonade,' he conceded.

'It's all right,' said his brother, in a rare moment of taking the initiative. 'He's no longer underage.'

Crocker's brow cleared. 'Oh yes, Rod does come in for the occasional beer.'

Major Bricket was well aware of the subtext here, that the boy had been served in the Goat & Compasses before he was eighteen. He salted away the information – the Major salted away all information – but he did not follow it through at that moment.

Instead, he continued, 'I've been trying to piece together what happened to Rod immediately after Sylvia died. I was busy abroad for the best part of two years round then.'

'Inspecting all those five-star hotels,' said Crocker knowingly. 'Nice work if you can get it, eh?'

Major Bricket had no idea what the landlord was talking about but put it down to the Devil's Burp. He went on, 'I heard rumours that Rod got into some bad company round then, went a bit wild.'

'I heard that, and all,' Crocker confirmed.

'Do you know who he was mixing with?'

'It'd be some gang from the school.'

'Which school?'

'The comprehensive, over Duckton way.'

'Might Rod have spent time with Danny Linton there?'

The landlord looked uncomfortable. 'I don't know. Maybe. He wasn't there long, though.'

'He was there for at least three years. He was there when Sylvia died.'

'Suppose he was. Then, suddenly, this bursary or whatever-it-was came through and Rod was whisked away to some posh boarding school.'

The Major could have pressed Crocker harder but didn't. Not the moment yet for the third degree. 'And do you know where Rod was living at the time?'

To his surprise, his question was answered by Derek Fosbury. 'Straight after Sylvia died, Rod lived with me and my missus, Bella.'

'What?'

'I think it might be easier,' said Derek with unexpected dignity, 'if you and I was to continue this conversation through in the main bar. We can talk with less interruptions there.'

And, leaving his gobsmacked brother gaping at the bar, Derek Fosbury led the Major out of 'Crocker's Corner', closing the door behind them.

Such a happening in the Goat & Compasses was unusual, maybe even unprecedented.

This main bar was mercifully empty, the good weather once again strengthening the allure of the pub's garden. Since they'd both just drained their glasses, Major Bricket ordered two more pints of Devil's Burp. He was served by the cheerfully long-suffering Mel Fosbury, whom he congratulated on the enduring high quality of her fish pie. Though she didn't say anything, it was clear that Mel was taken aback by the sight of Derek unaccompanied by her husband. The Major wondered idly whether, in the course of her married life, she had ever seen the two of them apart.

Mel retired to the kitchen to supervise orders from the garden and the two men had the place to themselves. They exchanged 'Cheers' and both took long swallows of Devil's Burp.

The Major kicked off. 'So, you say Rod actually lived with you?

'That's right.'

'I'm talking just after Sylvia died.'

'That's when it was. Well, it seemed only natural, with us being next-door neighbours, and all.'

'Oh, I knew you lived close, but I didn't know it was that close.'

'Yes, me and the missus lived right next door to Sylvia and Rod . . . well, and Jim till he scarpered. You haven't met my wife, Bella, have you?'

'No, I haven't had the pleasure.'

'Lovely woman.'

'I'm sure she is.'

'Anyway, like I say, Bella had always been in and out of Sylvia's place a lot, you know, drinking coffee, nattering and what have you. And when Sylvia got ill, Bella would take Rod into our place, you know, look after him. Take him to the hospital to visit his mother, and all. See he was getting proper meals. Then, after Bella passed, the boy stayed with us for a few months.'

'Was that official? I mean, did Social Services know about it?'

'Oh yes. There was nothing illegal going on. Because we had been close friends with Sylvia and, you know, neighbours, nobody worried. I think the social workers were glad of it as a short-term solution. It gave them a few months to sort out some kind of fostering arrangement for Rod.'

'There was never any question of his staying with you on a long-term basis?'

'No, Major. Bella and I were both still working back then. With the best will in the world, we just couldn't have done it.'

'So how long was Rod with you?'

'I suppose about three months ... well, four if you count the time while Sylvia was in hospital.'

'And then he did go to foster parents?'

'Yes.'

'Their name was Root.' They were getting up to the part of the story Major Bricket already knew about.

'Rod ended up with a family called Root,' said Derek, 'but that wasn't the first place Social Services put him.'

'So, who did he go to first?'

A slight cloud crossed Derek Fosbury's face. He seemed unwilling to say more, so the Major prompted, 'Might I know their names?'

'Ronald and Eva Wilkinson. Ronald's always known as "Nipper".'

'Local?'

'Yes. Live right here in Stunston Peveril. Nipper's an antiques dealer ... well, he was. Think he's retired now. But Rod was only with them for, like, six months.'

'Why was that? Why was he moved away?'

Derek's lips pursed wryly. 'It was thought that Nipper was an unsuitable guardian for a teenage boy.'

'Oh?'

'There were accusations against him of criminal activity.' Reading the question in the Major's eyes, he said hastily, 'No, nothing like that. No kiddie-fiddling. Nipper was accused of burglary. The case never come to trial – cops hadn't got enough evidence to pin it on him. But the view round Stunston Peveril was that Nipper was as guilty as hell. Anyway, the fact that the accusation against him had been made at all convinced the Social Services that perhaps he was an unsuitable role model as a foster parent.'

'So, then Rod was moved to live with the Root family?'

'That's right. And they was very good to him. Vicky Root's a lovely woman. Very kind. So's Bob, and all. Got a boy round Rod's age, two lads get on well together. Rod's still living there now. He's of an age to be beyond fostering, but the Roots like having him around, so that all seems to be working out all right.'

'Good.' Thanks in part to Nga Luong's research, Major Bricket already knew about Rod's domestic set-up. 'And they don't mind about the fact that he hasn't really got a job?'

'I asked Vicky about that once. She said, because of the trauma what he'd gone through with losing his mother, it was no surprise that he was taking a while to settle. She also said she thought she owed him.'

'How does that work out?'

'Well, when Rod suddenly got that grant – "bursary", I think it was called – it took him out of the local comprehensive and into this posh boarding school, Vicky Root said, due to some admin cock-up, she and Bob was still getting paid their money for the fostering. You know, during term times when Rod was away at school and not costing them nothing. So, they reckoned they owed him for that.'

'A very generous way of looking at the situation.'

'I agree. But then that's Bob and Vicky all over, isn't it?'

'I don't know. I haven't met them.'

'Loveliest couple you'll ever see.'

'Then I look forward to meeting them.'

Mel Fosbury appeared from the garden. 'You two all right for drinks?'

'Fine, thanks.' They'd been so involved in the conversation that their pints had hardly been touched. 'Derek, do you know any more about the time Rod spent with Nipper Wilkinson?'

'Nope. Nothing.' The words came down like a shutter. No more would be forthcoming from Derek Fosbury on that subject.

'Couldn't help overhearing,' said Mel from behind the bar – serendipitously, from the Major's point of view. 'Nipper Wilkinson and Eva used to bring Rod into the pub with them. They liked the Sunday lunch.'

'Yes, I have fond memories of it,' said the Major. 'As I recall, the pork crackling was well up to the standard of your fish pie.'

'Thank you.' Mel almost blushed. 'After poor Sylvia passed – and after Rod had been with you and Bella, Derek – Nipper and Eva used to come here Sundays with him. I remember, the drink the boy liked was cloudy lemonade. Had a good appetite, and all. No child's portion; he ate the full roast and all the trimmings.'

'That must've been while they were fostering him?' the Major checked with Derek.

He got a slightly unwilling nod. For some reason, Derek Fosbury didn't like talking about Nipper Wilkinson.

'Mel,' asked the Major, 'when the Wilkinsons had Sunday lunch here, was it just the three of them? Or did they meet other people?'

'Every now and then they'd meet up with Smiler Harrison. And quite often Noel Palgrave'd join them.'

'Sorry? Neither name means anything to me.'

'Noel Palgrave's a local art dealer. Got a house here in Stunston Peveril. Two houses, maybe... Sorry,' said Mel, hearing a shout from the garden, 'must get some orders out there.' And she disappeared into the kitchen.

'Do you know this Noel Palgrave, Derek?'

'Know who she means. See him around the village. Never talked to him. Bit up himself, I reckon. Ponces around in a cravat. Never trust a man in a cravat, I say.'

'And what about Smiler Harrison?'

'Very rarely see him. Small-time burglar. In the nick more often than not.'

'Have you ever seen him here in the pub with Rod Enright?'

'No.'

'But you have seen Rod here with Noel Palgrave?'

'A few times,' Derek replied cautiously.

'Any idea what the connection might be between them?'

Derek didn't sound very certain, as he replied, 'Don't know. Maybe a lawn-mowing job? Like Rod does for you?'

Like Rod does very inefficiently for me, the Major thought.

'I think there might be something else, Derek. Perhaps they—'

There was a noise as the landlord irrupted from 'Crocker's Corner'. 'Derek, I'm sure you've been chatting for quite long enough.'

'Quite long enough,' said Derek, back in his role of echo.

And Major Bricket knew he wouldn't get any more information from that source that day. Still, he had accumulated quite a useful supply of the stuff.

In the Goat & Compasses' phone booth, there was still an old-fashioned telephone directory, of the kind Massive Mazzini might well have torn up in his act. Both Nipper Wilkinson and Noel Palgrave's local numbers were listed. They probably used mobiles for most of their calls, but both landlines rang when Major Bricket called them.

A recording told him that neither Nipper nor Eva Wilkinson was currently available but offered him the option of leaving a message. He declined the invitation.

Noel Palgrave answered the phone. The Major was not specific about what he wanted to discuss but the art dealer readily invited him to call round. Presumably, he saw an opportunity to shift a Reynolds or a Lawrence (possibly of doubtful provenance . . . ?).

'This Major Bricket is becoming a little tiresome,' said the Employer.

'In connection with Danny Linton's elimination?' suggested the Employee.

'Precisely.'

'That's rather unfortunate.'

'It will be for him,' said the Employer. 'And I still haven't forgiven you for the total cock-up you made over the murder.'

'Not a total cock-up. The boy's dead, isn't he?'

'You know exactly what I mean. The significance of the murder was completely lost because of your mistake. It didn't send the message I wanted to send to the person I wanted to send it to.'

'I'm sorry,' said the Employee, not for the first time. Then, moving away from that uncomfortable subject to what might be a more appealing one, 'So, do you want me to do something about this Major Bricket?'

Rather than a reply, there was a thoughtful silence.

'If you do,' the Employee went on, 'can we forget the fancy dress this time? That clown suit made the job a lot more difficult. Having to steal one from Fincham Abbey, I could have got caught, easy.'

'It was necessary. And the scheme would have been highly effective, if you hadn't screwed things up so totally.'

Forgiveness was hard-won from the Employer. And, when the words were spoken with such conviction, the Employee knew better than to provide any follow-up argument. Indeed, argument of any kind was not to be recommended. A level of harmony could only be maintained by doing exactly as one was told.

But a follow-up question was permissible. 'So, do you want me to eliminate the Major?'

'Not yet,' said the Employer. 'Just keep an eye on him for the moment. If he shows signs of getting close to the truth ... well, that could ruin the whole operation.'

The Employee nodded agreement. 'But, when I get the word from you, I should be ready to eliminate him instantly.'

'Of course,' said the Employer.

7

The Art Dealer

'You're lucky to catch me,' said Noel Palgrave. 'I will be moving in just a few weeks.'

'Leaving Stunston Peveril for good?'

'Yes, I have retired, you see.'

'Me too,' said the Major. 'And there's nowhere I'd rather retire to than Stunston Peveril.'

'Ah. Well, there we differ.' The art dealer looked at him curiously. 'We haven't met before. Does that mean you have only recently moved to the village?'

'It means that I have owned a house here for more than twenty years, but my work has involved a lot of travel, so I've rarely been here.'

'That would explain it. Well, Major, I have been in Stunston Peveril every day of my working life and I cannot wait to leave the place.'

'Where are you going?'

'The Cayman Islands. I've had a property out there for some years. Near West Bay. And I'm longing to be spending all my time in the Caymans.'

'Will you be sorry to give up all this?' The Major gestured round the sitting room in which they sat. When the Major had arrived, Noel Palgrave had told him that this was not the house he lived in. It was one he had set up to display the artworks in which he dealt. Which explained Mel Fosbury's reference to his having two houses.

'Clients,' he explained, 'prefer to see paintings on the walls of a house, rather than in a gallery. It gives them a better idea of how they will look in their own homes. They can match colours and things.'

Major Bricket would not have claimed to be an expert on art, but the dealer's words gave him the firm impression that Noel Palgrave sold artworks more as a branch of the interior design business than for their artistic excellence. The paintings on display in his showhouse reinforced that idea. The Major had seen quite a few in the hallway and more in the sitting room where they sat. All were pleasant to look at – peaceful sylvan scenes, calm seascapes, portraits of ladies featuring winsome beribboned bonnets and a lot of white lace – but all seemed to be the work of a journeyman rather than a genius. They were done 'in the style of' more talented artists.

Noel Palgrave seemed to read his thoughts. 'As you may observe, I do not sell Great Art. I sell art people like to put on their walls to suggest they have taste. Many of my clients are clubs and hotels – particularly the international chains – who like to give their clients a sense of antiquity.'

'But the items you deal in are all genuine paintings of the period? Not knock-offs by contemporary artists?'

'Certainly not. I do have my integrity . . . though many in the art world would not recognise it as that. In art, as in everything else, Major, there are the winners and the also-rans. The winners have unique genius and their works sell for hundreds of millions. But there are many more also-rans, whose perfectly adequate works can be picked up very cheaply at auction by the discerning dealer.'

'A "discerning dealer" like yourself, Mr Palgrave?'

'Exactly.'

'And, if you are about to move abroad, what will happen to the array of artwork here?' His words were spoken with a gesture that encompassed the whole house.

'In the hall you may have noticed some parcelled-up paintings due to be air-freighted to a client in the Princedom of Qajjiah. It's in the Middle East.'

'I've been there,' said Major Bricket. But then, of course, he had been everywhere. He was also acutely observant and had checked out the details on the labels of the parcels in the hall as they passed through.

'I noticed,' he continued, 'that the packages were addressed to the Minister of Culture in Qajjiah.'

'Yes.'

'Wouldn't he be more interested in valuable paintings for display in a gallery, rather than "also-rans" for hotel rooms?'

'You might think so. The way ministerial responsibilities are distributed in a country like Qajjiah differs considerably from what happens in the United Kingdom. There, the Minister of Culture deals with tourism as well as art galleries.'

'Yes. And I see the packages are to go air freight with Qajjiah Airlines.'

'I have found them to be very efficient in the past.'

'I'm sure.'

'Now, I have packed all the paintings in the rooms upstairs. And will soon have done these down here . . .' The art dealer gestured round the walls. 'The person who is buying this house will find the walls unadorned.'

'And that buyer will be using the place to live in rather than as a display house?'

'I've no idea. I have not asked the question. All that has been dealt with by the estate agent.'

'So, you are not selling the business?'

'No, Major. There are no plans for it to continue. The business lives and dies with me. As I said, I am retiring and that is the end of it.'

'I trust you got a good price for the house?'

'Very satisfactory, thank you,' Noel Palgrave replied slyly.

'What would happen if one of your clients were to find that one of the paintings you sold him as an "also-ran" was discovered to be the work of an Old Master . . .?'

'There is no danger of that eventuality, Major. I am very good at my job. I would recognise anything really valuable.'

'Good.' The Major smiled a smile of complicity. 'Meanwhile, all over the world, hotel guests are waking to the sight of one of your original "also-rans"?'

'Exactly so.'

'I'm sure you fill an important niche in the art market.'

'Oh, I do, Major. My business has been very kind to me over the years.'

Major Bricket thought, If it's bought you a place near West Bay on Grand Cayman, then I don't doubt it.

But what he said was, 'I've come here to talk to you about a young man called Rod Enright.'

The art dealer's back stiffened almost imperceptibly.

'You know who I mean?'

'Yes, of course I do, Major.'

'I just wondered how you came to know him?'

'As I'm sure you're aware, Stunston Peveril is a very small place. Most people know each other. I think I first saw Rod Enright in the Goat & Compasses when he was quite young.'

'Would that be with your friends, Ronald and Eva Wilkinson?'

Noel Palgrave tried, unsuccessfully, to hide his shock at the detail of the Major's information. 'Yes, I suppose so,' he replied, forcing a calm demeanour on himself.

'Did you know, Mr Palgrave, there had been suggestions that Nipper Wilkinson had a criminal past?' There was no reply. 'A history of burglary perhaps?'

'I never listen to village gossip,' came the disdainful reply.

'That is, if I may say so, very short-sighted of you, Mr Palgrave. Among all the dross, a lot of useful information circulates in village gossip.'

'I'll have to take your word for that, Major.'

'What about Smiler Harrison? Have you ever seen him with Rod? Or with Nipper Wilkinson, come to that?'

'I've never heard the name you mentioned.'

The Major felt sure Palgrave was lying, but realised that a change of tack was needed. 'Since seeing Rod Enright in the pub as a youngster with the Wilkinsons, have you subsequently met him there on his own?'

'Possibly.'

'What? You arranged to meet him there?'

'No. For heaven's sake! There's nothing sinister going on here. The Goat & Compasses is the hub of village life. So, there have been occasions when I happened to be there at the same time as Rod Enright. Along with a lot of other people. I'm sure the conversation was general, and he and I just got talking.'

'This was recently?'

'I have seen him in the Goat & Compasses recently, yes.'

'And what did you talk about?'

'As it turned out, he was looking for work, and I suggested he might help with mowing my lawn. He told me he did the same at Highfield House while you were away on your foreign assignments.'

Major Bricket reflected on the ways of Stunston Peveril. He and Noel Palgrave had never met before, and yet the art dealer knew his address – and no doubt espoused one of the many village theories as to what he used to do for a living. Or maybe the art dealer had his own theory.

The Major looked out of the sitting-room window to the small, paved courtyard behind. 'It might be thought churlish of me to mention it, Mr Palgrave, but you don't have a lawn.'

The art dealer was, however, ready for that one. 'This house, as I told you, Major Bricket – had you been listening – I use only as a showcase for the artworks on sale. I actually live elsewhere in the village.'

'Of course,' said the Major, gracefully acknowledging his error. 'And did you find Rod efficient as a mower of lawns?'

'Perfectly adequate,' came the curt response. Which told Major Bricket that Rod had never been near any garden of Noel Palgrave's.

'And now,' said the art dealer, 'with my imminent move and all these remaining pictures to pack up, I am quite busy. Also, the questions you're asking seem to have very little relevance to me. I would suggest, if you want to know about the activities of Nipper Wilkinson and Rod Enright, rather than wasting my time, you should talk directly to the two individuals involved.'

The Major's considerable experience of interrogation always told him when he was not going to get anything else out of an information source.

He also recognised the truth of what Noel Palgrave had said. He relished the idea of a dialogue with Nipper Wilkinson. The one he must inevitably have with Rod Enright he relished less.

There were a few late lunchers lingering in the Green Lotus Restaurant, but the Major was being fed in the kitchen. Nga Luong had highly efficient local girls to act as waitresses, though they looked very English. Most Thai or Vietnamese restaurants in England are family-run, but Nga, having been transplanted on her own into the middle of Suffolk, could not use that kind of resource to get staff whose looks matched her own.

Her Suffolk girls, however, knew the menu inside out and could pronounce most of the items on it. Their ethnicity did not lead any of the Green Lotus's customers to feel that they had been cheated of 'the authentic Thai experience' (though in fact what they were getting was 'the authentic Vietnamese experience', served by English waitresses).

And it was the authentic Vietnamese experience that Major Bricket was lunching off in the kitchen. On the 'Specials' board in the restaurant that day was 'Thai coconut chicken curry', though he recognised it as 'Vietnamese coconut chicken curry'. He found it as delicious as he had when Nga Luong first cooked it for him in the backstreets of Hanoi.

He was about to raise the subject that had brought him to the Green Lotus, when one of the waitresses summoned Nga out into the restaurant. A customer had requested a fortune cookie. The Major could hear quite clearly the exchange that followed. A young man who was eating on his own told Nga Luong that he was terribly undecided whether, after seventeen years of cohabitation, he should ask his girlfriend to marry him.

The restaurant owner gravely pronounced his fortune. 'In all streams, flat stones are flatter than round stones.'

The customer thanked her ecstatically for the advice. He would go and put it into practice immediately.

Major Bricket was pleased to see a rare grin on the face of The Human Fortune Cookie as she came back into the kitchen.

'I have been making some progress on young Rod's past,' he said.

Nga Luong nodded thoughtfully. 'I could see last night that he wasn't telling us everything.'

'No. I'm sure there's some connection between him and the murder victim, Danny Linton.'

'They were at school together for a while, weren't they? Two schools, primary and secondary.'

'Yes. I'm sure there's something more, though.'

'But you say you're making progress.'

'I hope so. I need your help, Nga.'

'Always happy to oblige, Major.'

He spooned up the last of the delicious sauce from the Vietnamese coconut chicken curry. 'When you first moved here, you said that to keep your investigative skills up to speed, you were going to build up dossiers on everyone in Stunston Peveril.'

Nga Luong reached to produce a laptop from under the counter. 'Yes, I like to keep my hand in.' She opened the screen. 'Who do you want to know about, Major?'

'I wonder ... do you have anything on Nipper Wilkinson?'

A broad smile creased Nga Luong's normally impassive face.

'Oh yes, Major. Indeed I do.'

Although he was obsessed by information, Major Bricket knew when to hold back from asking where it came from. In the case of Nga Luong, out of admiration for her remarkable abilities, he never questioned her about the methods she used for obtaining the data she produced for him. If she chose to volunteer how it was done, then fine. If she didn't, he respected her secrecy. (And, in many cases, the fewer people who knew about how she did it, the better.)

In this instance, she did reveal something of her *modus operandi*.

'I've accessed the online bank accounts of Ronald Wilkinson, commonly known as "Nipper",' she said. He didn't ask how. 'There are quite a lot of dealings with Noel Palgrave.'

'Good.'

'Substantial sums received from him and substantial sums paid out to him. I can provide copies of the statements if you like.'

'Not necessary at this point.'

'There are various substantial amounts paid to other

individuals, but regular monthly payments to someone called "A. J. Harrison". I've done some research on him.'

Again, Major Bricket didn't ask how. 'Of course you have,' he said.

'Small-time crook,' Nga went on. 'Extensive prison record over the years, generally short sentences for burglary. Known in the criminal fraternity as—'

'Might I interrupt, Nga, and suggest he is known as "Smiler Harrison"?'

'Well done, Major. He used to live at various addresses in the Suffolk area ... that is, between prison sentences. Recently, though, he's upped sticks and moved to Portugal.'

'Ah.'

'But the interesting thing that the statements show is that, about four months ago, the regular payments to Harrison stop ... and a very large one-off payment is made from Ronald Wilkinson's account.'

'When you say "large" ...?'

'Three million.'

Major Bricket let out a low whistle. 'Intriguing.'

'Certainly is. And the payment coincided with Smiler Harrison's move to Portugal.'

'Even more intriguing.'

'I have spoken to Smiler Harrison and if you—'

Nga Luong was interrupted by the appearance of one of her waitresses. 'Another diner wants a fortune cookie.'

The restaurateur looked to the Major for permission.

'Yes, of course. You're giving me more gen than I could ever have hoped for.'

'What is it this time?' Nga Luong asked the waitress, as they moved through to the restaurant.

'Lady's dog died four months ago. She's stressing over whether she should get another one of the same breed.'

From the kitchen, Major Bricket heard The Human Fortune Cookie's latest pronouncement: 'The acorn that does not fall produces no oak trees.'

Once again, he heard the ecstatic reception that piece of oriental wisdom prompted. Then Nga Luong returned to tell him the details of her conversation with Smiler Harrison.

Earlier that same day, the Wednesday, Lord Piers Goodruff lolled in a throne-like chair, once sat in by a King of France, and looked out from the high windows of Highhouse Hall's Green Morning Room with satisfaction. He was master of everything he could see. He was master of the large number of black-uniformed staff who ran his stately home. And master of so much else besides.

He felt impregnable. He had taken on the British establishment at their own games and won them all. He had clawed his way into the country's aristocracy and had no intention of ceasing to claw. He had made some token gestures towards assimilating their manners and customs but, once he was established, took more pleasure in flouting them.

In his view, people who said money wasn't everything were just losers whose lips were pursed by all the sour grapes they had eaten.

He thought about everything that Highhouse Hall contained. All his. The Old Masters in the Long Gallery. The exquisite Louis Quinze furniture. The Venetian mirrors and chandeliers. The garage full of Rolls-Royces, Bentleys and Lagondas.

He didn't particularly like any of it. He had a range of experts who selected what he should buy. He had no appreciation of art. He just wanted to own more of the most expensive stuff than anyone else.

As Goodruff had these thoughts in the Green Morning Room, Murkish, in the way of the best butlers, manifested himself silently at the peer's side. 'Your morning whisky, milord,' he said in a voice that could have French-polished a Stradivarius.

Goodruff looked at the contents of the butler's Georgian silver tray. The decanter and ice bowl were also Georgian, as was the firing glass that he was to drink from. He would have preferred to drink from a tumbler, but his glass expert couldn't find one that was as expensive as the firing glass.

His whisky expert had failed. The Balvenie 50 Year Old the man had provided was not actually the most expensive single malt in the world (though a bottle still cost as much as the average family car). But since Lord Goodruff didn't know about the expert's shortcoming, he watched with appropriate relish as Murkish poured his drink.

The noble peer himself picked up a handful of ice and dropped it into the Scotch, thereby offending a large proportion of the Scottish nation, part of whose religion was that ice and a single malt should never meet. He then offended the rest of the Scottish nation, along with everyone else who likes whisky, by topping his glass up with Coca-Cola.

It was a characteristic Goodruff action, being deliberately offensive to accepted traditions. He preferred behaving like that to a much larger audience, but that morning he only had Murkish to witness his sacrilege.

And who could say what thoughts bubbled behind that impassive butler's exterior?

'Murkish,' the peer asked, 'have you heard about this murder over at Stunston Peveril?'

'I have indeed, milord.' Without ever being seen to ask for information, the butler did seem to have an encyclopedic knowledge of everything that was going on everywhere.

'Unusual case, wouldn't you say?'

'Unusual set-dressing, perhaps, milord. The clown costume and the iron bar. But the murder itself is probably quite mundane. Just one drug dealer sorting out a disagreement with another drug dealer.'

'Do you know for a fact that the murder was drug-related, Murkish?'

'It very frequently is these days, milord.'

'Yes.' Lord Goodruff downed the rest of his Balvenie and Coke and gestured that his glass should be refilled. Elegantly, the butler acceded to his request. 'Have you heard, Murkish, of a man called Major Bricket?'

'Would that be the Major Bricket who owns Highfield House in Stunston Peveril, milord?'

'It would indeed.'

'Then I know who you mean, but I have not met the gentleman. Nor do I know anything of his background.'

'Would you be able to find out something about his background?'

'I will give the matter my immediate attention, milord.'

'Excellent.' The noble peer consulted his stainless-steel Patek Philippe Nautilus Travel Time Chronograph. 'My morning mistress will be arriving shortly, Murkish.'

'Very good, milord. The Rose Bedroom is prepared, with the Dom Pérignon on ice.'

'Excellent. I am very impressed, Murkish, by the way you always know which of the bedrooms is the right one for which of my mistresses.'

'Thank you. But the task is just part of my job, milord. And it is really not difficult. The ladies themselves are well aware of which bedroom you entertain them in.'

'And, fortunately, there are plenty of bedrooms still unallocated for when I take on new mistresses.'

'Exactly, milord.'

'Which I would say, Murkish, is a very satisfactory state of affairs.'

'It does seem, milord, an excellent arrangement, so far as you are concerned.'

'I think I'll go to the Rose Bedroom now.' Lord Piers Goodruff moved towards the door. 'Oh, and I will be at home for lunch. Tell the chef I fancy caviar on ice. Followed by a Wagyu fillet steak.'

'Of course, milord. Will the lady be joining you?'

'God, no!' said the departing peer.

The mistresses were not relegated to the tradesmen's entrance, but there was a door specially allocated to them. Normally, one of Highhouse Hall's many black-clad housemaids admitted them, but that morning it was a job that Murkish insisted on doing himself.

So, when the relevant bell rang, he was ready to greet the new arrival.

He had seen her before, but the woman had only visited Highhouse Hall once, earlier that week. Lord Goodruff liked a good turnaround of mistresses, and another of Murkish's responsibilities was maintaining the flow.

Though none of the mistresses arriving at Highhouse

Hall gave their names, the butler knew this one. And, after letting her in, he'd given her a strong dressing-down for a serious blunder which, in his view, she had made.

Murkish had not actually seen a performance by Lavoisier's Circus, but he still knew the woman to be one half of 'Piotr and Petra – Facing Death Daily from the Razor-Sharp Knives!'

He also knew that she had come to Highhouse Hall for something far more important than sex.

8

Den of a Thief

Nipper Wilkinson lived in some style. There are lots of fine old original houses in Suffolk villages, where, over the centuries, there has been less rebuilding than in other parts of the country. Nipper's had been built by a fifteenth-century wool merchant and kept about it the air of a bragging local boy made good. Which was perhaps still appropriate. The half-timbered exterior, with its network of black beams, had been punctiliously maintained, and the sitting room into which Nipper's wife Eva ushered the Major was crammed with artworks and artefacts. The Wilkinsons certainly had an eye for quality.

Which was presumably why Nipper had been a success as an antiques dealer. Though he was now very firmly retired. That was one of the first things he insisted on at the start of his conversation with the Major. 'Completely given it up, I have. All my life I've been looking forward to spending more time with Eva and the dogs. Now at last I can do that.'

As if to provide a visual aid, at the feet of his armchair there sprawled two flat-coated retrievers, one black and one liver-coloured. Nipper Wilkinson projected the image of a man at peace with himself. He had had a respectable, busy and rewarding career and was now content, in his declining years, to settle for a quieter life.

How at odds that image was with the information Nga Luong had unearthed about him.

Major Bricket had only revealed a small amount of that information a short while before, when he fixed his meeting with the antiques dealer by phone (his second call had been answered immediately). But what the Major had mentioned had been enough to make Nipper Wilkinson agree very quickly to the suggestion of a conversation. So, behind the pose of bonhomie with which he greeted his guest – and insistence that he be called 'Nipper' rather than 'Mr Wilkinson' – there was an edge of anxiety. He watched the Major closely, trying to second-guess which way he would jump.

Eva Wilkinson, a woman to whom age had granted a serene amplitude, brought in coffee and, having dispensed it, took her place in another armchair, in expectation of a cosy chat.

That didn't last long. As soon as Major Bricket had said, 'I want to talk to you about Smiler Harrison', Nipper looked across at his wife and said, 'Weren't you going to put away the ironing, love?'

Eva, clearly no supporter of feminism, took her coffee and obediently left the room.

'What's this about Smiler Harrison?' the antiques dealer demanded. 'He shouldn't have talked to you.'

'He didn't talk to me,' the Major replied smoothly. 'A colleague of mine found out some information about him.' As ever, he was entirely confident of the accuracy of Nga Luong's research.

'OK.' Nipper tensed defensively. 'What is it?'

'Smiler Harrison has enough knowledge about your long history of criminal activity to have you sent down for a very long time.'

'But he's got his villa in Portugal,' said Nipper, as if this somehow invalidated what the Major had just said.

'Modern communication systems do enable one to contact people in other countries.'

'I know that! Don't get lippy with me!'

Unruffled, the Major said, 'I should point out, Nipper, that I have nothing to do with the police. I have no interest in getting you arrested for the crimes you have undoubtedly committed. All I want from you is information.'

'But, if I don't give you that information, then you might feel differently about shopping me? You're blackmailing me with what you might do if I don't spill the beans. Aren't you?'

'How accurately we seem to understand each other, Nipper.'

The antiques dealer, though not totally reassured by this exchange, did relax a little. 'All right. What do you want to know?'

'I'm interested in the experience you and your wife have of acting as foster parents?'

'Oh yes?'

'I wonder... maybe she should be back here to answer these questions. She was presumably as much involved in the fostering as you were?'

'No,' Nipper snapped. 'We leave Eva out of this.'

'Very well.' Major Bricket paused for a moment, marshalling his thoughts. 'I'm interested in the time when you and your wife fostered Rod Enright.'

The name had an effect, but he masked it well. 'I

remember him. Of course I do. Still lives somewhere round the village, I believe.'

'Yes, he does. I knew his mother, Sylvia. Did you?'

Nipper shook his head. 'No. The boy came to us after she died. He was only with us a few months.'

'I know that. And he was taken away by Social Services because there were some accusations of criminality against you.'

'"Accusations",' the antiques dealer repeated forcefully. 'Only "accusations". They never proved anything against me. A lot of unfounded accusations, but they were never able to make anything stick.'

This was pronounced with considerable pride. And the Major reflected that he too might be proud if the lavish lifestyle on display had been funded by crimes which he had got away with.

He didn't let such thoughts sidetrack him, though. 'Nipper, according to information from Smiler Harrison, you took a part in Rod Enright's education.'

'Well, obviously, the boy was finding it difficult to concentrate at school, you know, having just lost his mum, so Eva and I did what we could to help and—'

'That's not what I mean – and you know it's not what I mean.' Major Bricket was coolly authoritative. 'You taught Rod Enright the basic skills of burglary.'

'You have no proof of that.'

'If Smiler Harrison chose to talk, I think we'd have plenty of proof.'

'Just bloody greedy some people are.' Nipper Wilkinson sounded genuinely aggrieved, as if he'd been the victim of a serious betrayal. 'We did a deal. Smiler got the villa and a substantial cash sum, and the deal was—'

'I know. A cool three million.'

The art dealer gaped. How on earth could his visitor know that?

'Nipper, doing deals with fellow criminals has always been a procedure fraught with risk. People who break the law are not always dependable in their personal dealings.'

'I always have been,' asserted Nipper, apparently unaware that he'd just identified himself with 'people who break the law'.

Again, the Major was direct. 'How did you plan to use Rod's skills as a burglar?'

'It wasn't burglary. It was more, sort of, teaching him about issues of security ... you know, which windows people were likely to leave open. How it's often the window of the toilet, you know, because of the smell, and how someone small enough can climb through a toilet window as easy as pie.'

'So, did Rod Enright climb through some toilet windows for you ... in the course of his ... lessons on security?'

'Well ...' Nipper squirmed. 'Not that many.'

'You are in effect admitting that you used Rod to do burglaries for you.'

'Hardly burglaries. It was more like a game, just, you know, developing his skills. I'd set him up with friends of mine, seeing if he could break into their houses. A useful skill for a young boy to have.'

Nipper Wilkinson, Major Bricket reflected, was beginning to sound like Fagin, training up a thieves' kitchen of small boys. 'And that was all it was? Just getting Rod to break into the houses of your friends?'

'Well, just occasionally, it might be a bit different. I mean, say, for instance, I knew there was stuff in some big house that was valuable . . . but the owners didn't know it was valuable and they didn't appreciate its artistic value either . . . and I thought it would make more sense that the artwork should belong to someone who had more genuine appreciation for it . . . then I might organise a transfer of ownership. That's all,' he concluded lamely.

'So, you would get Rod – and maybe other boys you and Eva fostered as well – and you would order him to steal some artwork . . . which you would then sell on "to someone who had more genuine appreciation for it"? Is that how the system worked?'

'Well . . .'

The Major gestured around the room. 'And that's how you funded all this?'

He had been rather improvising, casting his fishing line of conjecture over the waters, but he was delighted to get a bite from his angry quarry. 'Here. How much did Smiler tell?'

'A surprising amount,' the Major lied. Then he cast out another fly-line of conjecture. 'And I've just come from talking to Noel Palgrave.'

A momentary stiffening, then, 'Oh yes?'

'Shortly to retire.'

'So I heard.'

'You've known him for a long time, Nipper.'

'Yes. That's the way it is in a village like Stunston Peveril. Everyone knows everyone.'

'Of course. And there would be a natural affinity between the two of you, with him as an art dealer and you an antiques dealer.'

'If you like.' Nipper was still unsure where this was going.

'Noel Palgrave also seems to have done very well for himself.'

'Clearly good at his job.'

'Just as you have been.'

'Thank you for the compliment.'

Major Bricket changed direction again. 'Presumably, some houses are easier to burgle than others?' he asked abruptly.

'I imagine that to be the case.' Nipper Wilkinson loftily dismissed the suggestion that the question might have any relevance to him.

'Fincham Abbey would, I imagine, be easier than most.'

'I have never been there,' said Nipper Wilkinson.

'Oh, you'd like it, I think,' the Major assured him. 'Somewhat run-down, with a great many neglected artworks hung randomly on its walls.'

'Really?' The antiques dealer feigned lack of interest.

'I had the good fortune to be invited to the costume ball there on Monday . . .'

'Did you?'

'. . . and I was looking at the display of paintings in the Great Hall.'

Nipper didn't think this worthy of comment.

'Some of them were a lot dustier than the others.'

'It's very difficult to get reliable cleaners these days.'

'So I've heard. And do you know, when I looked at those paintings, a bizarre thought came into my head. I wondered whether the less dusty paintings might have been replaced by copies . . . ?'

'As you say, Major Bricket, a bizarre thought.' Nipper

Wilkinson smiled magnanimously. 'A very bizarre thought.'

The Major knew it was an invitation that Rod Enright would not refuse. The glee he'd seen in the boy's eye the first time he'd been handed a gun guaranteed that.

In the Highfield House garden, he allowed his young guest to witness and marvel at the opening of the shed floor, and then led him down into the private sanctum. This time he wasn't careless; he closed the overhead ceiling to avoid another unexpected visitor.

That done, he gestured to the closed locker which contained his armoury of rifles and pistols. 'Thought you might like to try shooting with one of the other guns.'

'And how!' said Rod. 'The Smith & Wesson Model 14 .38 Special was good, but I'd really like to have a go with the Glock 27 G5 ... and the Ruger Mark IV. And the Colt New Service revolver ... I mean, I know it's quite old-fashioned now, but I'd really like to handle it.'

'Yes, it's still a great gun.' Major Bricket looked curiously at the boy. 'Are you sure you've never been down here before?'

"Course I haven't. I didn't know this place existed until I came in on Tuesday.'

'Then how did you know what guns I had in the locker here?'

'Well, I saw them on Tuesday, didn't I?'

'Only for a few moments.'

'Maybe.'

'But you recognised them and are able to remember all the details?'

'Yes,' Rod replied casually, as the achievement wasn't a big deal.

But Major Bricket recognised what a big deal it was. Having someone with a photographic memory on his team would be a bonus for any private investigator.

He let Rod watch as he unlocked the arms locker and the ammunition drawer. But he used his hands to cover the padlocks on the guns when he keyed in their relevant codes. He trusted Rod, but there were some pieces of information the boy did not need to know.

The Major himself didn't do any shooting. He allowed the boy the run of his gallery. Let him try the handguns he had remembered – and a few others. Still targets, moving targets, the range of the range.

What was striking was that, with every weapon, Rod showed the same prowess as he had on his first attempt. He was a natural shooter.

For a moment, Major Bricket wondered whether Rod had told him the truth when he'd said he'd never fired a gun before and got all his skills from watching movies. The Major was now fairly certain that Nipper Wilkinson had taught his foster child how to burgle. Had he taught him other criminal skills as well?

After an hour which was probably the most enjoyable of Rod's young life, the Major said that was enough. He showed how the guns should be locked away, though he still did not go as far as sharing the codes that held them secure. He then turned to another wonder of modern technology, an Italian coffee machine. He asked the boy how he took his, and soon the pair of them were sitting side by side at the control desk with steaming cups in front of them.

Major Bricket was, as ever, direct and to the point. 'Rod, you know more about the murder of Danny Linton than you have been letting on.'

The boy didn't argue.

'And you knew him better than you've been letting on too, didn't you?'

'Maybe. A bit.'

'Not when you were at Stunston Peveril Primary School?'

'No.'

'But when you were fostered by the Wilkinsons?'

'All right, yes.'

'Because you were at the comprehensive school at Duckton then, weren't you?'

'Yes.'

'Where you re-met Danny Linton?'

Rod nodded.

'And what – he bullied you?'

Another nod.

'Bullied you, just for the sadistic pleasure of it? Or bullied you to make you do something for him?'

'The second. Danny was already into drugs by then. Both as a user and a dealer. He was acting as a courier.'

'Contact with "county lines" people?'

'That's right. He was trying to get me into the business.'

'By bullying?'

The memory was still painful. 'Yes. And I was very close to doing what he wanted me to. But then suddenly I heard about this bursary, and I was whisked away to boarding school. I never understood how that worked. You didn't hear anything about the details, did you, Major?'

A firm headshake. 'Not a thing.'

'I haven't seen Danny from that moment to this.' A shadow was cast over his thoughts. 'And now I never will again.'

'No.' The Major pursed his lips. 'I'm coming round to the view that Danny Linton's murder was drugs-related.'

'Quite possible. I think he was still deeply into that stuff.'

'Well, look, presumably you've still got friends locally who knew Danny better than you did?' Rod nodded. 'Any information you can get out of them about him . . . I'd be very grateful.'

'Of course. I'll ask around.' The boy sounded eager, glad to be able to offer something positive, something other than apologies.

'Going back to when you were fostered by the Wilkinsons . . .'

'Yes?' That memory wasn't a welcome one to Rod either.

'You'd better tell me what happened.'

'Very well.' Rod seemed relieved actually to be talking about the subject. 'When I was with the Wilkinsons, Nipper was very nice to me. At least, he was very nice to me when I did what he wanted me to do.'

'Which was . . .?'

'He . . .' The boy hesitated.

'I have talked to Nipper. Needless to say, he wouldn't admit to anything, but I have a pretty shrewd idea of what he was up to.'

'What did he say?' asked Rod, still unwilling to reveal more than he had to.

'He talked of teaching you about security,' said the Major.

'Oh yes?'

'Teaching you about which windows might be open in a house, the best ways to get in.'

'Ah.' All resistance seemed to seep out of the boy.

'I think you know what I mean,' said the Major.

A rueful nod.

'So, which buildings did Nipper get you to break into?'

'He didn't call it "breaking in".'

'I'm sure he didn't.' The Major was relentless. 'Which buildings?'

'Nipper told me terrible things would happen to me if I ever told anyone about—'

'Rod, you're talking more than four years ago. When you were a frightened little fourteen-year-old. Nipper Wilkinson has no hold over you now. Nor, for that matter, does Danny Linton.'

'Well . . .'

'Tell me.'

It came out in something of a flood. 'He showed me how to get into Fincham Abbey. And Highhouse Hall.'

'The first one fairly easy. The second a bit trickier,' the Major observed.

'You can say that again.'

'So have you broken into both of them?'

'Fincham Abbey I did. Nipper was setting me up to break into Highhouse Hall – he'd done all the stuff of making plans of the interior layout – but then suddenly I had to leave the Wilkinsons.'

'And go to the Root family?'

Rod nodded. 'Funny,' he said, 'back then I kept getting "Highhouse Hall" mixed up in my mind with this place.'

'Ah. I can see that. The two names are quite similar.'

'Well, yes. And Mum used to mention "Highfield House" quite a bit, because she often came up here.'

'Most people in the village,' said the Major diplomatically, 'have been here.'

'Been *here*?'

'No, Rod, not down here. Not in my sanctum. You and Nga Luong are the only ones who've had that privilege. I meant that most of the inhabitants of Stunston Peveril have, at some point or another, been into Highfield House.'

'Oh yes. But Mum used to say—'

Major Bricket moved the conversation swiftly on. 'Going back to your burglary training ... tell me what Nipper told you to do once you were inside Fincham Abbey. Did he tell you to steal stuff?'

'No.' Rod was aggrieved. 'I wouldn't have done that. I remembered what my mum had always said about stealing. I was never going to do anything illegal.'

'Didn't you regard breaking and entering as "something illegal"?'

'No. Not if it was in the cause of justice.'

Major Bricket looked puzzled. 'Rod, could you explain to me, please, in what possible way breaking and entering Fincham Abbey could be in the cause of justice?'

'Nipper told me there were suspicions that the Viscount and Viscountess were in possession of some stolen paintings.'

The Major didn't ask why Rod had believed such an obviously ridiculous story. At the time, he had been a severely traumatised boy of fourteen, who probably believed that all grown-ups were honest. With the possible exception of his father.

'So, what did Nipper want you to do?'

'I had to break in, night-time, with a torch.'

'Through an open toilet window?'

'Yes. Bit of a squeeze, but I managed it,' he said with remembered pride. 'Nipper had done a map for me of the inside of the building. He worked out maps of quite a lot of buildings, particularly the really big ones in the area. He gave me copies of those, which I memorised. And he told me where in Fincham Abbey I'd find the paintings that had been stolen.'

'And, once you'd got inside the building, what did you have to do then?'

'I had to point my torch at the paintings and take photographs.'

Major Bricket nodded. 'And then take the photos back to Nipper . . . ?'

'And he would identify which were the stolen ones, yes.' Again, a hint of pride that the boy had done what was required of him, 'in the cause of justice'. 'He had an art expert to help him identify the stolen ones.'

'I bet he did. And I bet that expert was called Noel Palgrave, wasn't he?'

'Yes, he was. And, actually, when Nipper was training me, he challenged me to see if I could break into Noel Palgrave's house. You know, with them being friends, it was a kind of game.'

'I see. You say you still have copies of the burgling maps Nipper Wilkinson made?'

'Yes.'

'Bring them along next time we meet.'

The Major sat back, nodding with satisfaction. Inside his brain, conjectures were hardening into certainties.

9

Fake Value

Nipper Wilkinson might have had his own art expert in the form of Noel Palgrave, but Major Bricket was not without comparable resources. It hadn't slipped his mind that one of the subjects which had engaged Nga Luong's interest since she arrived in England had been English painting of the seventeenth and eighteenth centuries.

He rang her the next morning, the Thursday, and she readily agreed on a visit to Fincham Abbey. Though the Wintles had lunched occasionally at the Green Lotus Restaurant, they showed no signs of recognising her. But then they were both very short-sighted.

Perpetua ushered them into the Yellow Morning Room and offered coffee. Due to lack of staff, she had to go off and prepare this herself, leaving them to listen to the world-view of her husband.

'The trouble with things today,' Viscount Wintle began, 'is that people don't have values and, as a result, nothing has any value. Oh, there's financial value, of course, but that's one of the least valuable ways of valuing anything.

'I mean, value implies order, and order implies people knowing their place. I don't want to sound like a right-wing fogey' – which was ironic because that was exactly what he was – 'but I think the basic principle of socialism – that everyone should share everything equally – is an appalling way of organising things. It is a fact that very few people are born knowing how to run a country estate. A skill like that only comes from generations of breeding. So, if everyone in England had a country estate – which, if you follow the logic through, is what the socialists are asking for – there would be a lot of very badly run country estates.'

Major Bricket was aware of certain basic flaws in the Viscount's logic, but he had far too much breeding himself to mention them. It was a relief, though, when the Viscountess appeared with the coffee and he and Nga Luong could move legitimately on to the purpose of their visit.

'You have a very fine collection of paintings here, don't you?' the Major observed.

'Family stuff,' said the Viscount dismissively. 'Portraits and some oils brought back from Grand Tours, you know how it is.'

'Of course. Must be a hefty insurance bill.'

'So I believe. Such payments, I am told, leave one's bank account automatically these days.'

Perpetua, alerted by the vagueness of his reply, demanded, 'Gregory, you have kept the insurance up, haven't you?'

'Of course I have, my love.'

The airiness of this response did not convince either the Viscountess or their guests that the insurance was up to date. But, before Perpetua could remonstrate with her husband, Major Bricket asked, 'Would you mind if Miss Luong and I were to have a look at some of the paintings in the Great Hall? She is doing some research on seventeenth- and eighteenth-century English painting, and it would be very useful for her thesis.'

Nga Luong did not even flicker an eyebrow. She was accustomed to the Major inventing lies to explain her presence in a variety of situations (mostly considerably more hazardous than the present one). And she did have a genuine interest in seventeenth- and eighteenth-century English painting.

'No. Please go through, by all means.' The way the Viscountess said this suggested that she would be glad to have them out of the room. And the persecuted expression on the Viscount's face suggested he'd rather they stayed. He knew he was about to be taken to task for not keeping the insurance up to date.

Major Bricket was acutely aware of when silence was required, and he was silent while Nga Luong inspected the paintings in the Great Hall. Even in daytime, the lighting from the stained-glass windows was inadequate but, always prepared for every eventuality, Nga Luong had a torch and magnifying glass with her.

She didn't rush. She gave every picture a generous amount of scrutiny and made notes on her phone. Only occasionally did she touch the surfaces to check some detail of the brushwork.

Eventually, she turned to face the Major and announced, 'Seventeen of them are copies.'

'Good copies?'

'Not bad. Good enough to fool the casual viewer.'

'And certainly good enough to fool a pair of elderly, short-sighted aristocrats?'

'No problem.'

'And are the frames copies too?'

'No, original frames. Well, frames that have been there at least a century, anyway.'

'Which means replacing them must have been quite a lengthy process?'

'Certainly.'

'Let's start at the beginning of the process, Nga. As I told you, Rod Enright was being trained to break into this house and take photographs of certain paintings. Copies must then have been made . . . and I wouldn't be surprised to find out that Noel Palgrave organised that part of the scheme. Then someone with some basic skills in framing technique has to come here and replace the originals with the copies . . . a job which would certainly take quite a long time.'

'It would,' Nga agreed. 'And looking at the frames, the substitution has been quite well done. I can't see any scratches or other signs of disturbance. What do you think the security's like in this place?'

'Minimal. The Viscount and Viscountess keep complaining about their lack of staff, and I don't know how many of them – if any – sleep in overnight. The Wintles' bedroom – or bedrooms, one never knows with people of their age and class – are presumably a long way away upstairs. No, after dark, once the crook with the copies had broken in, I don't think he'd be in much danger of being disturbed while he did the substitutions.'

'He wouldn't have had time to do more than a couple of paintings a night,' Nga reckoned.

'I get the feeling this whole process has been done over quite a few years,' said the Major. 'That way the crooks're less likely to be caught and the substitutions are less likely to be noticed. Just a gradual process of stripping Fincham Abbey of every valuable painting it possesses. Nice work if you can get it.'

'And what do you reckon happens to the originals after they leave here?'

'I don't know, but I'm pretty certain Noel Palgrave might have that information.' The Major made a mental note that the interior of the art dealer's display house might be worth another visit. Preferably when the owner wasn't there. And those packed-up paintings he'd seen in the hall, destined to go to the Minister of Culture in Qajjiah – what was all that about?

'Do you want to look in the rest of the house?' asked Nga. 'I'm sure there are more paintings in other rooms.'

'No, this gives us enough to be going on with. An accurate inventory can wait till the case is over.'

'And when will that be?'

'Soon,' said the Major with grim determination.

'Do you want to go and tell the Wintles what we've found?'

'No. Let them spend a little longer in blissful ignorance. We will just go and thank them for the coffee, and for the way they have helped with your research into seventeenth- and eighteenth-century English art.'

'Very well.'

'Letting them know about our findings can also wait until the case is successfully concluded. No point in upsetting the old dears unnecessarily. We can tell them the news about the thefts at the same time as we identify the perpetrators.'

Nga Luong chuckled. 'Nice idea.'

'Incidentally, how are your researches into the business connections going?'

'Well, but slowly.'

'Not too slowly, I hope. We need to get everything wrapped up before the end of Saturday.'

'We will,' said Nga Luong.

'Excellent,' said Major Bricket.

Viscount Wintle had no interest in gardening, but when the two visitors returned to the Yellow Morning Room, they were informed that he had 'gone out to look at things in the garden.' Major Bricket was of the view that he had in fact gone out to escape the wrath of his wife about the unpaid content insurance on Fincham Abbey.

But, of course, Perpetua would never have admitted to outsiders that she and Gregory ever disagreed about anything. Instead, she beamed widely and offered them more coffee. The Viscountess could never be faulted on social niceties.

Nga Luong had to go back to open the Green Lotus Restaurant, but she told the Major she would forward to him the latest research she had done on her laptop the previous night. She also said that, if he fancied discussing the case in the restaurant kitchen again, the Thursday Special was Thai (well, in fact, Vietnamese) barbecue pork asparagus fried rice.

Taking in this information, Major Bricket walked briskly back to Highfield House.

In his sitting room, checking through the data he'd just received by email from Nga, he was alerted by a tapping on the French windows. He looked up see a very nervous-looking Piotr, the knife-throwing half of Petra and Piotr.

When the door was opened, the man rushed in, as if in fear that he was being followed. He brushed some leaves out of his hair.

'I am sorry,' he said in his heavily accented English. 'I come from the circus through woods. I do not want people see me.' He looked impassioned as he continued, 'Major Bricket, Massimo is a friend of mine. I cannot let him suffer. He did not kill the boy!'

'I know,' said the Major coolly.

'But he is arrested. He could get a life sentence for murder.'

'That won't happen.'

Piotr was not so easily reassured. 'Circus people – the English police always suspect circus people. Particularly if they are foreign. Because Massimo is not English, he will not get a fair trial.'

'He won't go to trial,' said the Major soothingly. 'Because very soon I will have proof of who actually did murder Danny Linton.'

'Who is it?' demanded Piotr.

'I don't know yet.' Major Bricket turned his interrogator's eye on the man. 'Do you?'

Piotr looked uncomfortable as he replied, 'No, I do not know.'

'But maybe you know why he was killed.'

The knife-thrower wrestled with some counter-arguments before replying, 'I think I might know the reason.'

'Drugs?' the Major suggested.

Piotr looked flabbergasted. 'How do you know this?'

'Everything seems to point in that direction. I've found out that Danny Linton was a user of drugs – and a dealer, too. People in that world think nothing of killing anyone who they think is cheating them.'

'No. That is true.' The man's tone suggested he knew from his own experience.

'Piotr, I want to ask you about the business of Lavoisier's Circus taking on temporary staff at each of the stops on their touring schedule.'

'It is bad idea, no?'

'Why do you say that?'

'Lavoisier's Circus used to be made from families. All families, all know each other. Then Bernard, he decide, no. That is not the way. Now he run circus with extra people brought in. They know nothing about circus life. Everything – setting up Big Top, taking it down – takes longer because they do not have the practice in doing these things.'

So far, this confirmed exactly what Camille Lavoisier had said. The Major asked, 'Do you know why Bernard made the change?'

The knife-thrower shrugged. 'This is something we in circus ask ourselves a lot. Why would he do this? Perhaps, we think, because he is old man and drunk. His brain is not good now. So, he do stupid things . . .?'

The Major pursed his lips. 'I don't think that explains it. What he did would have taken a great deal of planning and organisation. It's not something that could be set up by someone who was losing their faculties. I think Bernard must have been acting under pressure from someone else.'

'Perhaps. In the circus we have talked about this possibility.'

'Any idea who that "someone else" might be, Piotr?'

'I don't know. Maybe Camille? She seems running everything now.'

Major Bricket remembered how forcibly the ring mistress had denounced her father's change of staffing policy for Lavoisier's Circus. But then, she could have been lying. In the course of his varied career, the Major had encountered many very convincing liars. For the first time, the question came to him of whether Camille Lavoisier was as straightforward as she had seemed to be.

But he didn't share that thought with Piotr. 'You must have seen a good few of the "temporary staff" who helped out at other stops on the tour?'

'I have, yes.'

'Were they good workers?'

'Not lazy but, like I said, they did not know job they had to do.'

'I just wondered . . .' A theory was crystallising in Major Bricket's mind '. . . whether they, like Danny Linton, had anything to do with drugs?'

'I think possible, yes.'

The Major nodded. The knife-thrower looked uneasily out into the garden. 'I must not stay. People wonder where I go.'

By 'people' the Major felt pretty sure he was referring to his domineering wife.

'You'd better get back then. But don't worry about Massimo. I guarantee that he will be released as soon as the real murderer is unmasked.'

Piotr nodded with relief. Somehow he intuited that Major Bricket was not a man to offer his guarantee and then not come up with the goods.

Piotr was in such a rush to cover the open ground between Highfield House's French windows and the shelter of the trees that he did not notice the figure watching from the edge of the wood.

It was his wife, Petra. Her expression was unforgiving.

Though they hadn't spent much time together since they had been in the same class at Stunston Peveril Primary School, Rod Enright and Ferdy McNeile knew each other. In a small village, it was hard for people not to know each other. They would nod and wave if they passed in the High Street and exchange a few words in the Goat & Compasses.

So, it was not totally incongruous that Rod should suggest they meet in the pub for a pint. He didn't give the reason for his suggestion until they were sitting opposite each other in the main bar, two pints of Devil's Burp in front of them. Both took long, satisfied slurps before Rod got on to the purpose of their meeting.

'I wanted to talk about Danny Linton.'

'Poor bugger,' said Ferdy. 'I know his life was a bit of a mess, but no way did he deserve to lose it like that.'

'No,' Rod agreed.

As ever, Ferdy McNeile looked amazingly healthy. Well over six foot tall, he was as brown as a berry. The strength of his upper body strained against his plaid shirt. He had never been in a gym in his life. His muscular development came from outside work on the family farm.

'You were the same year with him at Duckton Comprehensive, weren't you?' asked Rod.

'That's right.'

'Mates?'

Ferdy McNeile grimaced. 'Not close. Well, there was a time when we were. Used to mess around in class together. Neither of us had much time for school.'

'Just didn't like authority?'

'I think it was that with Danny. He just liked creating hell. For me, well, it was more that I was bored. I couldn't see any time in the future when the stuff they were teaching us was going to be of any use to me. From the moment I was born, there had never been any question. I was going to work on the farm and take over from my dad when he kicked the bucket.'

Ferdy read the question in Rod's raised eyebrow. 'No, the old man's still with us. Strong as a mule – and as stubborn. So, anyway, I didn't bother with school. Left as soon as I legally could – and had been doing a lot of truanting before that. You know, come harvest, Dad needed me. The farm always came first.'

Rod felt a little jealous of the certainty in his former schoolmate's words. Despite having absolutely no desire to be involved in farming, he wouldn't have minded having some kind of life plan at such an early age. A plan to do something. A plan to do anything.

'And was Danny into the drugs back when he was at school?'

'Oh yes, you bet.'

'Did you ever get involved?'

Ferdy looked around rather shiftily. Reassured that they were alone in the bar, he thought it safe to answer.

Even so, he spoke in a whisper. 'I did a bit. Went to a few parties with Danny, where some stuff was going on. I did some weed – and cocaine. Might have continued down that route. Danny never seemed to have a problem sourcing the stuff. But one Sunday morning, after I'd been out late the night before, Dad wanted some help forking vegetation into the silo, you know, to make silage. And I was so out of it, I was completely useless. Dad knew the reason and he gave me such a major bollocking that, since then, I've stuck to legal substances. Beer, that's my only vice now.'

'And a very fine one,' said Rod, raising his glass in salute and taking a long swallow of Devil's Burp. 'Did that also mean you saw less of Danny?'

'Yes. He wanted me to get involved in the dealing and there was no way I was going down that route.'

'Did he bully you to try to persuade you?'

Ferdy McNeile flexed his huge biceps and grinned. 'No. Danny didn't try to bully me.'

The moment brought back bad memories for Rod, along with another pang of jealousy. Maybe if he'd had more physical bulk, he could have stood up to his tormentor.

'Do you have any idea, Ferdy, what Danny did after he left Duckton Comprehensive? Did he stay around the area?'

'So far as I know, yes. I'd see him around from time to time. In here, sometimes, but then I think Crocker banned him for peddling drugs.'

'That would figure. Did he ever have a job?'

'He kept trying stuff. I heard that from some of his mates. I mean, Danny was quite talented, good with his hands, I remember. Art class at Duckton, he kept making obscene clay models of staff members. Got in a hell of a lot of trouble for it, but the actual models were pretty good. I was envious of his talent. So, I think he tried a few jobs, but none of them lasted more than a couple of weeks. You know, he'd be stealing the stock, have his hand in the till, be offensive to customers. I don't think Danny was cut out for full-time employment.'

'And you don't know if there were any jobs he did for more than a few weeks?'

'Well, there was one,' said Ferdy.

And he revealed what it had been.

Their short acquaintance had told Rod how much Major Bricket liked to have facts backed up by evidence. So, he went straight to the building in Stunston Peveril High Street where Danny Linton had been employed and he asked the proprietor how good the young man had been at the job.

The Major was gratified when Rod passed on the information. Apparently, the owner of the Magpie Gallery had appreciated Danny's skills and was annoyed at having to sack him. But the scam the young man was practising with customers' credit cards left him with no alternative. It was a pity, because people with a natural aptitude for picture framing were hard to find.

Major Bricket was extremely pleased. The list of people who might have wanted Danny Linton dead was lengthening by the minute.

He was also pleased that Rod Enright had remembered to bring copies of Nipper Wilkinson's burglary maps.

10

Time for Truth

Eating the Daily Special in the Green Lotus Restaurant while discussing murders was a bonus afforded to few private investigators. Major Bricket was aware of the privilege. He found the Thursday Special of barbecue pork asparagus fried rice just as good as everything else that came out of Nga Luong's kitchen.

Cooking was so instinctive to her that she could meet the constant orders brought in by the waitresses and still discuss the minutiae of the research she had done overnight for the Major.

'I looked at what you sent me,' he said. 'I'm very impressed by the way you manage to get into private bank accounts.'

'I hope you're not going to ask me how I do it.'

'Nga, I wouldn't dream of it.'

She grinned as she plated up two portions of Thai (i.e. Vietnamese) caramelised pork belly with fermented shrimp paste for one of the waitresses to deliver.

'I feel we're getting close,' said the Major.

'Not quite close enough, though.' A one-frame expression of frustration crossed Nga Luong's face. 'There's such an impenetrable network of companies, it's hard to get back to who actually owns them. I'll find the answer, though,' she concluded with determination.

'I'm sure you will. But don't forget, we still have a deadline. Lavoisier's Circus leaves Stunston Peveril on Saturday night.'

'I'm well aware of that, Major. And there's no other way you think you can get the information?'

'I do have a couple of thoughts, yes. I'm sure Camille Lavoisier hasn't told me everything she knows. And her father's hiding something, too.'

'But how're you going to—?'

She was interrupted by one of her waitresses. 'Sorry, Nga, but someone's just asked for a fortune cookie.'

'Have they said what the problem is on which they need guidance?'

The waitress dropped her voice to a whisper. 'It's a woman who wants to know whether she should continue going out with two men, neither of whom knows about the other.'

'Not a local then,' murmured Major Bricket.

'How do you know?

'Nobody could keep that kind of two-timing a secret in Stunston Peveril.'

'You're right.' Nga Luong grinned at him. 'Excuse me a moment.'

Taking another large mouthful of the delicious barbecue pork asparagus fried rice, the Major listened to the exchange in the restaurant.

'You are the one who wants a fortune cookie?'

'Yes. I read about the "special service" in a Tripadvisor review.'

So, news of The Human Fortune Cookie was spreading.

'Do you want me to tell you the problem about which I need advice?' asked the woman.

'No,' said Nga Luong. 'The message from the fortune cookie is stronger if I do not know.'

'Very well.' The voice was urgent now. 'What is it? What is my fortune?'

Nga Luong made her sombre pronouncement: 'For the sea snail, his shell is big, but the sea is not.'

'Oh, that's wonderful!' said the woman's voice. 'You've made everything clear for me!'

In the kitchen, Major Bricket grinned.

It was about half past one as he approached the Goat & Compasses. As before, the pub garden was filled with families stoking up on Mel's excellent food before the two thirty performance of Lavoisier's Circus. The Major made his way straight to 'Crocker's Corner'. Predictably enough, the two Fosburys and Bernard Lavoisier were in their established places.

There was also a fourth person with them in the bar. Old, very tall, and almost skeletally thin, with wisps of hair sticking out of his liver-spotted cranium, he was introduced to the Major as 'Dr Hubert Devizes – better known as "The Great Pantherleo"!'

Neither name nor nickname was familiar to Major Bricket, but characteristically he bought a round of drinks for all present. Three pints of Devil's Burp, brandy for Bernard Lavoisier and . . .? He asked Dr Hubert Devizes what he would like.

'Just a fizzy water for me, please,' the old man replied. His voice was that of a desiccated academic, precise and formal. 'Back when I was working, I never dared to have an alcoholic drink, for reasons of safety, and I'm afraid the habit – or, perhaps, lack of habit – has stayed with me.'

'Don't apologise,' said the Major. 'I wish I could say the same.'

As Crocker pulled the pints, Major Bricket asked, 'So what was it you did, Doctor, when you were—?'

'Please don't call me "Doctor". Everyone knows me as "Pantherleo".'

'Very well then, Pantherleo ... what was the job you did, for which you needed such a steady hand? Were you a surgeon?'

There was a chuckle from the two Fosburys, who knew exactly how the question would be answered.

'Not a surgeon,' the old man joined in the chuckle. 'But I was in a business in which there was also a strong possibility of bloodshed. I was a lion-tamer.'

'Ah.'

'Hence the name – "The Great Pantherleo".'

'As in *Panthera leo*?' The Major was quite good on the Latin names of animals.

'Exactly!' The old man nodded eagerly, pleased to have the reference picked up. The Major wondered what subject the doctorate had been in.

'Not many around now in your line of work,' he observed.

'No. More's the pity. A whole profession destroyed by over-sensitive people who thought we were actually harming the animals.'

Major Bricket looked sceptical. 'I think there was quite a long tradition of circus animals being bullied into performing.'

'Bullied by incompetent tamers, yes. The skilful ones – like The Great Pantherleo, I am proud to say – *persuade* a performance out of a lion.'

'Oh yes?'

'It is true.' He tapped the shoulder of the comatose circus owner. 'Bernard, tell him. You never saw me being cruel to an animal, did you?'

'No,' came the slurred response.

'See?' Dr Hubert Devizes splayed out his hands, as if his point had been incontrovertibly proved. 'Bernard and I have worked together for decades. He knows everything about me and I know everything about him. And he knows for certain that I would never hurt an animal. Isn't that right, Bernard?'

The circus owner, still more interested in his brandy than supporting his former colleague, appeared not to have heard the question.

'It is sad,' said the lion-tamer, 'that so many of the circus traditions have died. The skills used to be passed down within the family, father to son. For many years I felt sad that I had no children, that I did not have a son to pass down the lion-taming expertise to. Now I am glad it didn't happen. It would have been much worse to watch a son of mine gradually see the work drying up and all the excitement draining out of the circus life.

'Lion-taming is an honourable tradition which has been killed, along with so many others by simple pussy-footing – which is perhaps the appropriate word. Risk used to be the seasoning for all activities. Now Health and Safety rule. Do nothing in your life, in case the worst happens. It was the prospect of the worst happening that motivated us – that and the skill with which we prevented the worst from happening.

'But it's all gone now. As have so many other good things. Everything in life that used to give pleasure is now frowned on. And performing dangerous tricks with animals who positively enjoy showing off ... no, of course you can't do that. I wasn't even fifty when the Great Diktat came down. "No more circus acts with animals!" And suddenly I was out of a job.

'Trouble is, lion-taming is not really a transferable skill. When it was clear I wasn't going to get any more work doing what God intended me to do, I went to the Labour Exchange ... No, they don't call it that now. What is it? Job Centre, maybe? They ask me if I have any qualifications. I tell them I am "The Great Pantherleo, the World's Most Daring Lion-Tamer"! They suggest I should apply for a post teaching in a primary school. They keep bigging up the similarities between the two jobs, but I can't see it.

'For a while, I think it is only a blip. Soon, the world will come to its senses. They will realise the great void left in the entertainment business by the absence of animal acts. And, on his return to his proper place within the scheme of things, The Great Pantherleo will be greater than ever. I have kept up my skills, you know. If I had a call to go back into the ring, even after all these years, I'd be there in an instant.

'For that reason, at first I didn't get rid of my animals. Yes, I'm sure there are zoos that would have taken them, but they were family for me. The family I never had because I was so busy honing my skills as a lion-tamer. So, after I lose my job, I keep the animals. I do not have many back then – three lions and a couple of tigers is all. But keeping them in a suburban garden doesn't work out. My neighbours in Milton Keynes turn out to be very nit-picking about stuff like that. They make unreasonable complaints to the local authority about the noise and the smell.

'So, I sell up the house and buy a camper van. I also buy a big trailer with iron bars for the cats. But do I find people on campsites are more broadminded than the *petit bourgeois* of Milton Keynes? I do not.

'For some years, I travel round the country, but it is difficult to find places for the cats to get exercise. And life gets complicated when Deirdre, the lioness, gets pregnant. She has two cubs and space in the trailer is getting impossible. With great reluctance, I contact a zoo in Germany and drive out there with the animals. I won't spell out the pain of our parting. And, because they were by then of an age to leave their mother, I keep one of the cubs. For a few years, I tell myself. Then, that one too will go to the zoo.'

He sighed. 'I don't think lion-taming will ever return as a form of entertainment. Not in my lifetime, anyway. Perhaps, in the future, there will be people with more tolerant and forward-looking attitudes and . . .' The fantasy dried up. 'But I doubt it.

'Nothing is as good as it used to be.' He placed a bonhomous hand on the shoulder of the brandy-drinker beside him. 'That is why I have searched out my old friend, Bernard. To commiserate. I was driving the camper van through East Anglia and I see a poster for "Lavoisier's Circus". I've never heard of Stunston Peveril, but I found my way and – here I am!'

'You certainly are,' said Crocker Fosbury.

'Yes, you are,' Derek Fosbury agreed.

'And I am delighted to see, Bernard, that Lavoisier's Circus is still running, that you are still in charge.'

'I do my best,' said the circus owner. 'I am keeping up a long tradition.' He didn't assume his French accent. The lion tamer was too old a friend for such subterfuges to be needed. Major Bricket was interested by the change of tone, though. Up till that point, he had only heard pessimism from Bernard Lavoisier. Perhaps, in the company of his former colleague, he didn't want to lose face.

'Good for you,' said The Great Pantherleo. 'For keeping the show on the road. Last time I saw you, you were all doom and gloom.'

'Oh well, circumstances change,' said Bernard Lavoisier.

'You never spoke a truer word,' said Crocker Fosbury.

'No, you didn't,' Derek Fosbury agreed.

'And that girl of yours, Camille,' asked the lion-tamer, 'is she still involved in the business?'

'Oh yes. I rely on her a lot. Very good second in command.'

Again, a strikingly different analysis of their relationship from the one Bernard Lavoisier usually presented to the habitués of 'Crocker's Corner'. Major Bricket was intrigued. If they wanted to go on talking, he wanted to go on listening.

Particularly as The Great Pantherleo's next question was: 'And the finances? Did you manage to sort those out?'

'Yes, that's all fine,' said Bernard Lavoisier, in a tone implying they had exhausted that topic of conversation.

But the lion-tamer persisted. 'I remember, you were

talking about getting an outside investor to see you over that tricky patch. Carkvale Stuke – I think that was the name of the company you—'

'No,' said Bernard Lavoisier with some vehemence, 'I managed to get things back on track without—'

Who could say what further information the Major might have gleaned, had Camille Lavoisier not burst into 'Crocker's Corner' at that moment? She was resplendent in her ring mistress ensemble, and her face was as red as her coat from running.

'I may have to pull this afternoon's show!' she cried. 'Piotr's gone missing!'

11

A Knife-Thrower is Missing!

It turned out that the knife-thrower had not returned to his caravan after going out for a walk. No one knew where that walk had taken him, and Major Bricket didn't think it was the moment to mention their morning meeting at Highfield House.

According to Camille, Petra was totally distraught and unable to perform in the afternoon show (though what act she would have managed to do as one half of a knife-throwing duo was not specified).

After what had happened to Danny Linton, the circus company were all paranoid that some similar fate might have befallen Piotr.

Bernard Lavoisier, still in the new positive persona he'd assumed in the presence of The Great Pantherleo, had gone with his daughter down to Ratchetts Common to work out how they could rearrange the programme for the afternoon performance.

They were followed out of the pub by an overexcited lion-tamer, shouting, 'I can fill in the gaps! I can do my act! I've got a small lion in the camper van!'

Major Bricket stayed with Crocker and Derek Fosbury to finish his drink.

He texted Nga Luong and asked her to investigate a company called 'Carkvale Stuke'.

The news of Piotr's disappearance spread quickly through Stunston Peveril. And, equally quickly, theories were propounded as to what had really happened to him.

Elvira Finchcombe in the Gingham Tea Shop assured her customers that Piotr the knife-thrower was actually the murderer of Danny Linton. As he felt the police investigation closing around him, he had done a runner. He was, even at that moment, on a ferry from Harwich to the Hook of Holland.

Rhona in Cosy Collectibles stuck to her conviction that it was illegal immigrants. A group of them had been holing out in the woods near Ratchetts Common. Piotr had stumbled on their secret camp and he had been killed to stop him from shopping them to the authorities.

The suspicion that Lena who cleaned at the vicarage shared with the vicar's wife was similar to Rhona's, the only difference being that, rather than stumbling on the secret camp of illegal immigrants, Piotr had stumbled on the secret camp of a demonic cult. And it was they who had killed him to stop him from shopping them to the authorities.

Dierdre in the Post Office knew all these conjectures to be nonsense. Piotr, like Danny Linton, had tried to enter the chapel to steal the casket containing a piece of the True Cross. Predictably enough, the Knights Templar had had their revenge on him.

In the Goat & Compasses, Crocker Fosbury, needless to say, was convinced that Piotr had been abducted by aliens.

Derek Fosbury agreed.

In 'Crocker's Corner', Major Bricket felt uncharacteristically tense. He was anxious to hear the results of Nga Luong's research. He had also texted Rod and not yet heard back. A man of action never likes inactivity.

He went outside to put through a call to a long-saved number on his mobile. Vicky Root, Rod's foster mother, answered straight away. 'Hello, Major. Very good to hear from you. All well?'

'Pretty good, thank you. Just wondered whether Rod's around. I need to talk to him.'

'He's not in trouble, is he?'

'No, not at all. It's just . . . I texted and he hasn't got back to me.'

'He's at the gym. Building himself up for the start of the rugby season.'

'Excellent. Well, if you see him, could you ask him to give me a call?'

'Of course, Major.'

And he had to be content with that. Still feeling unsettled, he decided he could do worse than watch the afternoon performance in the Big Top again. Though elements of the case were falling into place, there was still a lot unexplained. And much of the unexplained stuff, he felt sure, had some connection to Lavoisier's Circus. Seeing the show again might prompt some new insight.

From the professionalism and cheerfulness of the ring mistress's demeanour, none of the audience would have known the kind of pressure she was under. Camille Lavoisier, once again, showed her complete control over the proceedings.

Major Bricket was intrigued as to how she would cover over the absence of Petra and Piotr. And he couldn't have been more surprised by what actually happened.

After the clowns' act with their collapsing car had proved to be as unfunny as ever, the ring mistress stepped back into the ring with her customary sexy aplomb.

'Ladies and gentlemen, we now have a change to your programme. Instead of the advertised artistes, you are going to have a special treat. You will be seeing an act which has not been performed for more than half a century! It's one of the classic routines in circus history. The generation who saw it first time round still speak of it in awestruck tones. Ladies and gentlemen, will you please give a big Lavoisier's Circus welcome to . . . Bernard and Hubert – The Plastered Plasterers!'

The costumes and props must have been assembled with remarkable speed, though none of them were objects that wouldn't be found backstage at a circus. The two participants, one thin as a sapling, the other round as a tuber, were dressed in white overalls and forage caps. They carried a long plank, two sets of folding steps and a ladder, all made of wood. Apart from this, all they needed were large brushes and buckets of whitewash. With, of course, plastic sheeting laid down to protect the floor of the ring, and to warn the audience to expect slapstick.

What was astonishing was how readily Bernard Lavoisier and The Great Pantherleo stepped back into their roles. Camille had not been lying when she said they hadn't performed together for over fifty years. But the routine was one that they had done so often, it was locked into their muscle memory. At the sketch's inception, Bernard and Hubert had been young men, pretending to be old and drunk. Now, neither of them needed to pretend to be old, and for Bernard to appear to be drunk required no acting at all.

Yet each move was as precise as a guardsman's drill. Every slip off a stepladder, every slop of whitewash from a bucket, every misstep on the paint-covered cloth, every thump from a plank, every collision of brush and face was exactly calibrated. It was like The Plastered Plasterers had never been away.

And the audience that afternoon in the Big Top on Ratchetts Common appreciated what they were being privileged to witness. The applause at the end of the act was long and loud. And the veteran performers were gratified to see that their antics were just as popular with the watching children as they were with the adults. The routine was a triumph.

The only people present who might have been less than enthused were Lavoisier's Circus's resident clowns. The Plastered Plasterers had only served to show how resolutely unfunny their own offering was.

Contrary to the ring mistress's injunctions to the audience before the performance, Major Bricket had left his mobile switched on throughout. Still nothing from Nga Luong or Rod. Major Bricket sent another text to the latter, copying into Vicky Root, asking him to call back and then go to Highfield House as soon as possible. Something important they needed to discuss.

Rather than going straight home, he again went round the back of the Big Top. If anyone had questioned his presence there, he would have said he wanted to congratulate Bernard Lavoisier and Dr Hubert Devizes on their stunning routine. But his real purpose was to talk to Petra about her husband's disappearance.

The first person he met, though, still looking magnificent in her ring mistress gear, was a very flustered Camille Lavoisier. She carried a large bunch of keys.

'Petra and Piotr's car has gone!' she announced, striding towards their caravan.

'That flashy Beamer?' asked the Major.

'Yes.'

'I thought you said they were very tight on security, always kept their place locked.'

'They do, but I have to have keys to all the caravans.' Camille checked through the bunch for the knife-throwers' one. 'In case of fire or some other emergency.'

'Of course.'

She had found the right key. The Major was pleased she was saving him the trouble of asking about Petra.

The opened door revealed a modern caravan interior, with no personal items evident. He got the impression it had always been that way. Petra hadn't just collected up all their memorabilia before she did a runner. They'd never had any memorabilia.

But Camille recognised that something was missing. 'My God! She's taken their props!'

Major Bricket knew what that meant. The spinning wheel onto which someone could be strapped. And a collection of twelve very sharp knives.

12

Break-In

Back home, the Major went straight to the bookcase in his sitting room. Ignoring the extensive library of books on church architecture, he took down a volume he'd never opened. A house-warming present from back when he'd first bought Highfield House. He couldn't even remember who gave it to him. It was called *Suffolk's Historic Homes*.

He was not interested in Fincham Abbey. He opened the section on Highhouse Hall. Early sixteenth century, the place was built by yet another successful wool merchant, whose family were staunch adherents to the Church of Rome. This made life rather uncomfortable after the accession in 1558 of Queen Elizabeth, who instigated wide-scale persecution of Catholics. During this period of paranoia, there was much suspicion of illegal masses being conducted in Highhouse Hall, but no proof could be found. So, the family survived through the Civil War and into the nineteenth century, when the property was finally sold to one of the emergent railway moguls.

The building, he discovered, had never been open to the public, but certain unique architectural features of the interior had been restored.

Major Bricket read the article with considerable attention. He compared the plan of the house's interior with the burglar's map which Nipper Wilkinson had given to Rod Enright. He was satisfied by what he discovered.

The research had been useful displacement activity, but the Major still couldn't settle till he had heard back from Nga Luong and Rod. He contemplated opening up the shed for more target practice, but didn't feel in the mood. The news of Petra's disappearance made him certain that events were speeding up, but that he had no control over their tempo. And, if there was one thing Major Bricket hated, it was not being in control.

Rod was first to break the telephone silence. As Vicky had said, he was at the gym (something of which the Major thoroughly approved) and had not seen his phone till after his shower. He said he'd come up to Highfield House straight away.

The silence broken, Nga Luong called very soon after. She had done a lot of research into the firm of Carkvale Stuke.

And yes, it had produced the result Major Bricket had been hoping for. He felt energised, once more back in control.

Waiting for Rod to arrive, he fancied one more turning of the screws on Nipper Wilkinson. He rang the number. The answering machine clicked in but, as soon as he mentioned his name, the receiver was picked up by a tense, even fearful, antiques dealer.

'What do you want?'

The reply came back in the Major's silkiest voice. 'Further to our delightful meeting yesterday ... I just wanted to say that I've just had another little chat with Smiler Harrison.'

'The bastard!'

'Yes, I'm afraid he wasn't very generous in what he said about you.' Major Bricket was talking complete nonsense. No call with Smiler Harrison had taken place. But he had been trained in the business of talking complete nonsense in an entirely believable manner.

All Nipper Wilkinson could come back with was another, 'What do you want?'

'I was talking to Smiler about the unfortunate Danny Linton.'

'Oh yes?'

'Small for his age, wasn't he? Like Rod Enright?'

'What if he was?'

'Well, I was just thinking that, when the Social Services stopped you from fostering Rod, that left you needing another small boy who could climb through toilet windows, didn't it?'

'Maybe.'

'You couldn't go down the fostering route again, but somehow you met Danny. He was a bit older than Rod, and less naïve about what you were asking him to do. He'd been on the wrong side of the law for most of his life. Already had a drug habit, so he needed the money. And when he developed the skills of picture framing at the Magpie Gallery – a job you probably set up for him – well, you were laughing, weren't you? You'd got the full package in one person. Danny could break into premises, take out the valuable paintings and replace them with the copies. Neatly into their original frames.'

'If you think,' said Nipper Wilkinson, 'that I'm going to admit to any of this . . .'

'I don't need you to admit. When the case is concluded, a dossier of all the relevant details will be sent to the police. How they choose to proceed with that information is, of course, up to them.'

'Look, Major, if you think you can pin Danny's murder on me, you're barking up totally the wrong tree!'

'I know that,' came the calm reply. 'You may have committed some crimes which are actionable, but murder is not among them. So, you can relax about that, Nipper, can't you?'

Major Bricket ended the call. He left the antiques dealer maybe relaxed about charges for murder, but not about any other kind. Which had been precisely his intention.

'I'm wondering how good your memory is, Rod.'

'Pretty good, I'd say.' Having seen the boy's detailed recall of the pistols in the shooting gallery, the Major thought that was probably an understatement.

They were in the sitting room of Highfield House where, earlier the same day, Major Bricket had heard a tapping on the window from the vanished Piotr.

'You know we talked about your time with Ronald and Eva Wilkinson, when Nipper was effectively trying to groom you into being a burglar?'

'I remember.'

'Has any of the detail stayed with you – you know, specifics of how to conduct break-ins?'

'I remember every detail. It's funny, but I think that time of your life, early teens, your mind is very receptive. It's like there were great long screeds of stuff we had to learn at school – the periodic table, things like that – and I still have instant recall of every word.'

'Hm. We'll put that talent to the test. You told me Nipper got you to break into Noel Palgrave's house, just for a game, because Noel was a mate of his?'

'Yes.'

'Well, how do you feel about breaking into Noel Palgrave's house again?'

Those summer evenings, it didn't get properly dark until nearly nine o'clock. Rod walked past his target a couple of times, to be sure that Noel Palgrave – or, indeed, anyone else – was not in residence. He had no worries about being seen actually doing the break-in. The route which Nipper Wilkinson had devised and trained him in using was through the small yard at the back. Access was by a latched door which opened on to a passageway behind the row of houses.

Rod didn't find it remarkable how vividly he remembered his previous break-in. In his case, it wasn't just that thing about instant recall of things you learnt in your early teens. It all came back to him because it was filed away in his photographic memory. He'd turned down the Major's suggestion of taking Nipper's map with him. Every detail was still crystal clear in his mind.

Earlier, in daylight, he had checked out the passageway. In the intervening years, CCTV might have been installed. But, mercifully, there was none.

Coincidentally, and unknown to either, Nipper Wilkinson had passed on to Rod a tip straight out of the Major Bricket playbook. When you're doing something secretive, always look as if you have a destination. So,

Rod Enright entered the dark passageway as if on the way to a hot date at the other end.

But there was nobody about to care how purposeful he looked. Perfect.

He lifted the latch with great caution, to avoid any alerting clicks. He pushed the door open and entered the backyard. Though the contents of the space had obviously changed, it was just about as tidy as it had been on the previous occasion.

Of course, the obvious danger was that the first thing Noel Palgrave might have done after Rod's first break-in would be to ensure that no one else could get in by the same route. But he'd said at the time that was so unlikely that he wasn't going to bother to make any changes. It was too improbable that anyone would repeat the routine.

Rod remembered vividly how that earlier escapade had ended. Having triumphantly made it, armed only with a small torch, into Noel Palgrave's sitting room, he had been totally panicked when the lights were switched on.

They revealed Nipper Wilkinson and Noel Palgrave, sitting in armchairs with glasses of whisky, which they raised to toast his success. They also offered him a drink, and so, at fourteen, that was the first time he had tasted spirits.

That memory also prompted the recollection of how simple the task had been. The challenge to break into the house had been more a test of his nerves than of his skills as a burglar. With the information Nipper had provided, he could hardly go wrong.

This time, he followed exactly the instructions he'd been given on the previous occasion. As he went through the process, he seemed to hear Nipper's briefing, word for word.

'Once you've got into the backyard, switch on the little torch I give you, but keep it pointing downwards. If you raise it up, people might see the beam. Go across the paving to the back door. To your left at the bottom of the wall you'll see an airbrick – that's like a brick that's got rows of holes in it, designed for ventilation. Push in the left-hand side of that. It'll move quite easily, and you'll see, attached to the exposed back of it, there's a metal box with a keypad on top. Key in the code "896532" and the box'll open. Inside it, you'll find a back-door key.

'Open the back door, raise your torch beam to the wall directly opposite and you'll see the burglar alarm display screen. If a red light shows, the system is on and an alarm will sound within thirty seconds. Key in the code "1945". A green light will replace the red light and the alarm will be disabled. Keeping your torch beam low, leave the kitchen, go into the hall, and enter the sitting room on your left. In there, you'll find a present for yourself.'

The 'present', of course, first time round, had been Noel Palgrave and Nipper offering their congratulations. And the whisky. Rod hoped he wouldn't encounter the same greeting this time. And he didn't. The house seemed to be comfortingly empty.

In the event, he didn't go as far as the sitting room. Major Bricket had told him what he was looking for would probably be in the hall.

There were no windows there and the front door was solid, so he now felt it was safe to switch the lights on. As Major Bricket had briefed him, piles of heavily wrapped packages were stacked up against the walls. They varied in size – the biggest with the proportions of a door, the smallest the dimensions of a laptop. He lifted one up. It was surprisingly heavy.

The labels on all the packages were busy with print. As well as the Qajjiah Airlines logo, there were a lot of codes and numbers and the words: 'Pre-checked by HM Customs', with an authoritative-looking stamp.

Using the Stanley knife that Major Bricket had told him to carry, Rod selected a middle-sized package and started to cut through the tape and bubble wrap which formed the outer layer. Outer layer of many, it seemed, as he cut further in. As he got nearer the contents, he inserted the knife with greater caution. He had a strong suspicion of what he'd find in there and didn't want to cause any damage.

As anticipated, what he took out of the packaging was a painting. Rod's knowledge of art was limited, but he could recognise that it was quite an ordinary painting. An anaemic landscape of a field with cows at the edge of the stream that ran through it. The kind of artwork that might be hung on the wall of a hotel room and hardly be noticed by the guests.

When he saw what the contents were, he was surprised by how heavy they felt. Still following the Major's instructions', he turned the painting over and inspected the back. A wire fixed to screw eyes was obviously there for hanging. Under that, the back was protected by a sheet of cardboard, whose edges had been fixed to the frame with pale brown tape. Careful as a surgeon with a scalpel, Rod used the Stanley knife to ease the covering off.

What this revealed was another bubble-wrapped

rectangle, fitted snugly against the back of the canvas. He lifted it out, his hands trembling with excitement.

More cautious work with the Stanley knife on the surface that had been facing him. The packaging slipped off.

And Rod Enright faced a painting which he recognised from some years before, when he had photographed it in the Great Hall of Fincham Abbey.

Also between the two paintings was what Rod identified as a legal document. Not knowing much about such things, he still managed to get the gist of its contents. It seemed that Gregory, Viscount Wintle had sold the painting for two point five million pounds to the Crown Prince of Qajjiah. Rod looked at the packages around him. What kind of prices had the other Fincham Abbey paintings gone for?

Major Bricket had instructed him to call when he had some evidence.

So, he did. He rang the mobile and told the Major what he'd found.

'Excellent,' came the gratifying reply. 'Put the two paintings back together as well as you can, and bring them as evidence. You've done a good job, Rod. Great to see you taking the initiative. Really justified your place in the team.'

At this accolade, the boy's heart could not have swelled more.

'I'm going to the Goat & Compasses shortly. Meet me there,' said the Major.

At the end of the phone call, Rod Enright just felt huge pride.

He looked at the package he had opened. Evidence! Evidence appreciated by Major Bricket, no less. Who had also appreciated how Rod had been 'taking the initiative'. Acting off his own bat. Making quick decisions at moments of stress.

Yes, he had got the evidence. But you can never have too much evidence, Rod reasoned. He decided to check whether there were more paintings that he recognised in Noel Palgrave's house. And what kind of mouth-watering prices they had gone for.

Nga Luong could have scanned the documents and emailed them to the Major, but she felt happier handing them over in person. Because of her own much-used skills in that area, she knew how easy it was to hack into another person's inbox.

Major Bricket poured large Scotches for both of them. As he knew from many drinks they had shared in Vietnam, while he liked to add ice when it was available, she didn't.

The first documentation she handed over was the long trail through Companies House data and other sources, which had led to the uncovering of who ultimately owned Carkvale Stuke, the institution that had possibly bankrolled Lavoisier's Circus. It added interesting detail to what the Major already knew.

Nga Luong's next piece of evidence was a photocopy of a newspaper cutting.

'In a further initiative to improve the tourist attractions in the kingdom, the Crown Prince has announced plans to build a National Gallery in Qajjiah. He said that it would rival such institutions as the Metropolitan Museum of Art, the Louvre, the Prado and London's National Gallery. Given the depth of Qajjiah pockets, we can look to the Crown Prince

soon becoming a very active player in the international art markets.'

The Major let out a low whistle. 'Well, that explains quite a lot, doesn't it?'

Nga Luong didn't look satisfied. 'What it doesn't explain, though, is why Noel Palgrave – and whoever he's working with – waited so long. Rod Enright was photographing the paintings when he was fourteen. Surely they didn't know back then that the Crown Prince of Qajjiah was going to announce the creation of a National Gallery four years later?'

'No, but I wonder whether this was a long-term strategy, a retirement plan, if you like. The two main people involved in the scam are, so far as we know, Nipper Wilkinson and Noel Palgrave. Nipper has retired, Noel's about to retire. They both seem to be very well-heeled – Noel Palgrave's got a place on the Cayman Islands, for God's sake. Maybe they've been sitting on the stolen paintings, just waiting to put the plan into action. They saw the Crown Prince's announcement and thought the timing was serendipitous.'

'Possible.' Nga Luong still didn't sound totally convinced.

'Well,' said the Major briskly, 'we'll find out when they are arrested.'

'Oh?' Nga Luong looked surprised. 'When will that be?'

'I'll call the police as soon as I know that Rod's out of Noel Palgrave's house. I've fixed to meet him at the Goat & Compasses. The police will soon have enough evidence to make life very uncomfortable for Nipper Wilkinson and Noel Palgrave.'

'You sound very confident, Major.'

'I am. And what's that other piece of paper, Nga?'

'Another newspaper cutting.' She handed across the photocopy. It was of a page from the *Daily Mail*.

Major Bricket read:

'I'm a winner and I live in a world where only winners survive. If you don't like competition, get out of the race. I started with nothing and everything I have achieved, I have achieved through my own efforts. I didn't get any parental leg-up on the ladder of life, like so many people I meet in what is called "the cream of British society". I have succeeded by my own efforts and on my own terms.

'And I don't apologise for the fact that I sometimes have contempt for the people who have got to the top from inherited wealth – they're just a bunch of clowns. I have contempt for their titles, their stately homes, their art collections, their shooting parties, their MCC memberships, their gentlemen's clubs, their air of superiority, their butlers. They're all clowns. I have all of that and I started with nothing. I can appreciate talent that makes money; I can't appreciate inheritance that takes money.'

Major Bricket was unsurprised to discover from the clipping that the person expressing his opinions so trenchantly was Lord Piers Goodruff.

13

Confrontation at the Goat & Compasses

Major Bricket got out the Midget to drive down to the Goat & Compasses with Nga Luong. He had a feeling the rest of the evening might involve a car journey.

Nga had no objection to the pub. She just very rarely went there. This was chiefly because the Goat & Compasses' most convivial times of day coincided with those when she was cooking for her customers in the Green Lotus Restaurant.

There were moments when even someone as disciplined in controlling his emotions as the Major could allow himself a little bubble of excitement. It was something he had experienced in his professional life: a sense that all the elements are coming together to create some kind of climax. And part of the thrill comes from the uncertainty, the knowledge that the climax still might comprise success or failure.

Having witnessed the afternoon show and seen how well the routine had gone down, he reckoned – in the absence of a strongman and a knife-thrower act – The Plastered Plasterers would be doing a repeat performance in the evening. He also reckoned that, having done his bit in the first half, Bernard Lavoisier would not be staying on for any curtain call. He would make straight for the Goat & Compasses. And, though not a drinker, there was a strong chance that The Great Pantherleo would be with him.

Once he'd parked the Midget, the Major checked his phone, just in case there was a further communication from Rod. He bore in mind the lack of signal in 'Crocker's Corner'. There was no message. The boy might well have reached the pub already. Or he'd arrive shortly.

The Major had worked out to a nicety what time The Plastered Plasterers' act would end, allowed for longer applause from an evening audience, and worked out how long it would take them to walk from Ratchetts Common to the pub.

Needless to say, he'd got it right. The main bar of the Goat & Compasses was full of Thursday night locals. In 'Crocker's Corner', it was much quieter. The landlord was just pouring out, respectively, a large brandy and a sparkling mineral water for the two circus artistes, when the Major entered with Nga Luong. Crocker pointed to the Devil's Burp tap. 'Pint of the usual, Major?'

'No, thank you. Large Scotches for both of us tonight.' He wanted to keep his wits about him. Who could say what the next few hours would bring?

Nga Luong took her ice-free whisky and sat back to observe. And to listen. Always to listen. She was at least as good as Major Bricket in melting into the background when the circumstances required it.

The Major leant across to the circus performers and asked, 'How did it go tonight?'

'Like a dream,' said The Great Pantherleo. 'Audience loved us.'

'Positively baying for more,' Bernard Lavoisier agreed.

Actors talk about 'Dr Theatre', the amazing spirit who gives the most exhausted or sick performers energy when they step on stage. It looked as though the good doctor had prescribed a dose of the right medicine for the circus owner. Bernard Lavoisier was transformed. Yes, he'd nearly finished his first brandy, but there was more sparkle in his eyes than Major Bricket had ever seen.

He wondered if it was just the afterglow of a successful performance, or was there some other reason for his becoming suddenly more relaxed.

'Excellent,' said the Major. 'Are you going to take it up again permanently?'

'Well, it's a thought,' said Bernard.

'Certainly is,' Dr Hubert Devizes agreed. 'I've wasted so much time waiting for lion-taming acts to come back into acceptability. I could do worse than spend my last few years doing The Plastered Plasterers routine. That is, if Camille would let us.'

'If she doesn't,' said the girl's father, with a bravado the Major hadn't witnessed before, 'she'll have me to argue with!'

'That sounds scary,' said Crocker Fosbury.

'Certainly does,' Derek Fosbury agreed.

'Bernard,' said the Major, 'there's something I want to talk to you about.'

'Talk away,' came the bonhomous response.

'It's something you might rather talk about in private.'

'What is it?' the circus owner asked suspiciously.

'The financial affairs of Lavoisier's Circus.'

To the Major's surprise, this was answered by a laugh. 'We don't have to do that in private. I'm among friends here. There's nothing I need to keep from them.'

'No, there isn't' said Crocker Fosbury, anticipating some juicy gossip.

'There certainly isn't,' said Derek.

Major Bricket was pleased by Bernard Lavoisier's willingness to talk in public. Given the Fosburys' local knowledge and Dr Hubert Devizes's recollections of Lavoisier's Circus in the early days, the three might have something of their own to contribute.

'All right.' The ice in his whisky tumbler clinked as he took a sip, nodded to Nga Luong and set out on his planned course. 'Bernard, when I was talking to Camille about the funding that's stopping the circus from going belly-up—'

'That's no business of hers,' her father protested.

'I think it is, since she's currently running the place.'

The circus owner didn't take issue with that, waiting to see what the Major might come up with next.

'She said she'd taken you to task on the subject many times, but you'd never told her where the money was coming from.'

'If I chose not to tell her, I would have thought that was my decision.'

'Oh yes. But fortunately' – the Major turned to The Great Pantherleo – 'you were kind enough to give me a clue.'

The lion tamer looked puzzled. 'Was I?'

'Yes. You mentioned "Carkvale Stuke".'

'Oh yes, Well, at one stage I heard Bernard saying—'

Lavoisier turned on the Major with an expression of contempt. 'And do you happen to know who Carkvale Stuke are?'

'As a matter of fact,' came the cool reply, 'I do.'

Major Bricket pulled out of the inside pocket of his jacket the printout of Nga Luong's investigation into the company. If anything needed spelling out, he was glad she would be there to provide the full story.

'I don't want to go through all the ownership details. There's a whole sequence of shell companies and all that kind of deliberate obfuscation. But my extremely efficient research team' – Nga Luong didn't flicker an eyelid – 'have managed to find out who the ultimate owner of Carkvale Stuke is.'

'Well, it's no news to me,' said Bernard Lavoisier. 'And I'm happy to tell anyone.'

'You weren't happy to tell your daughter.'

'Circumstances can change, Major. No, I couldn't tell Camille, because I was under intense pressure not to do so. But, now . . . what shall I say? That pressure has eased considerably.'

'So, who were you under pressure from?'

'The ultimate owner of Carkvale Stuke.'

'That makes sense. Who's going to say the name? Would you like to, Bernard? Or shall I?'

'I'm quite happy to,' the circus owner replied. 'Carkvale Stuke is owned by Petra Jankowska. Better known perhaps as Petra from Petra and Piotr, the knife-throwers.'

Major Bricket did not, even by the smallest twitch of a lip, give away the shock that this answer had given him. Nor did Nga Luong.

'And now,' said Bernard Lavoisier gleefully, 'she's

gone away! So, she no longer holds the threat of violence over me.'

'Violence? So that's how she controlled you?'

'Yes, at first it was all harmonious. She knew – everyone in the circus knew – how desperate our financial situation was. Petra took me aside after one particularly badly attended performance, when I was at my lowest. I'd just lost my wife and everything looked totally grim. Petra told me that she had inherited a lot of money from some Jankowski relative in Poland and set up a company to protect it. That company, for reasons never explained to me, was called Carkvale Stuke.'

'I remember you mentioning it,' said The Great Pantherleo.

Bernard went on, 'Petra said she didn't want the money to sit idle, so she acted as a kind of venture capitalist. Investing in start-ups and arts projects that she thought could do with a leg-up. Because of her long association with the circus, she thought Lavoisier's was the sort of project Carkvale Stuke should get involved in.'

'Very generous of her, wasn't it?' Crocker Fosbury observed.

'Very generous,' his brother echoed.

Major Bricket continued listening to Bernard Lavoisier, for all the world as if he was believing every word. Nga Luong remained impassive, as ever.

'Petra set the whole thing up through her lawyers. I just had to sign a few papers and it was a done deal. A large injection of cash into Lavoisier's Circus every month, with no strings attached.'

'Except . . .?' the Major prompted.

Bernard Lavoisier's face turned gloomy. 'Except that,

as time went on, there did seem to be more and more strings attached.'

'Like getting rid of some of the older circus members and taking on temporary staff in each venue you visited?'

Bernard Lavoisier looked shell-shocked. 'How on earth do you know about that?'

'I worked it out from some things your daughter told me.'

'Really?'

'Yes. And I assume,' the Major continued smoothly, 'that Petra would give you the list of temporary staff for each venue?'

The circus owner nodded.

'Did you know, Bernard, that those temporary workers were all using Lavoisier's Circus as a centre for their drug dealing?'

'I guess I probably did,' he conceded. 'But I closed my mind to it. I found, the more I drank, the less I noticed that kind of thing.'

'And you never told Camille any of this stuff?'

'No. Petra threatened that if I did tell Camille . . . And I knew she didn't make idle threats. I'd seen evidence of what she'd done to any of the temporary workers who stepped out of line.'

'Using the knives?'

'Yes.'

'Did you actually see her kill any of the workers?'

He shook his head. 'Left some of them with pretty nasty scars, though.'

Major Bricket then resorted to one of the oldest tricks in the Interrogator's Handbook. Corny, maybe, but it did sometimes still work. He said, 'Strange that she didn't use the knives when she killed Danny Linton...'

'Yes, I thought that,' said Bernard Lavoisier, falling straight into the prepared booby trap. Too late, he realised what he'd admitted. 'Ah.'

The Major pressed on, 'Did you actually witness the murder?'

'No. I saw Danny Linton follow Petra into their caravan.'

'This would have been on the Sunday, the day you arrived in Stunston Peveril?'

'Exactly. It was after dark, when we'd got the Big Top up, and while the rest of the company were in their caravans having something to eat, I saw Petra and Piotr coming out of theirs, carrying some heavy object wrapped in a rug. They took it to their car. When I heard about the corpse found in your garage, I knew what had happened.'

Major Bricket looked puzzled. 'I keep wondering,' he said, 'why they would have chosen Highfield House as the place to dump the body. Usually, in criminal circles, that kind of gesture is a warning to someone. Sort of "You're next!" threat. But, until Tuesday, I had never had anything to do with anyone from Lavoisier's Circus. So it seems counterintuitive.'

'Very,' The Great Pantherleo concurred.

'Ah well, it might not have anything to do with the circus,' suggested Crocker slyly. 'Maybe you offended some upmarket hotelier by the review you gave him. Could be that.'

'Could be,' Derek agreed.

The Major had no idea what they were on about. The Devil's Burp talking, perhaps? He turned back to Bernard

Lavoisier. 'And you've no idea why they might have put the body in my garage?'

'Not a clue.'

Major Bricket was getting the beginnings of a clue as to the explanation, but that wasn't the moment to share it.

'Anyway, what happened to Danny can't have made you any less frightened of Petra. If she could do that to one person who stepped out of line . . .'

'Exactly. That's why I've spent most of the week drinking in here.'

'Just one thing . . . The fact that you saw Piotr helping Petra with the body . . . did that make you think he might be part of the Carkvale Stuke set-up?'

'I'm pretty sure he wasn't. I did raise the subject once, but Piotr didn't have a clue what I was talking about. I think, like the rest of us, he just knew better than to disobey his wife.'

Though the circus owner had got a lot wrong, he had still supplied some useful information. The Major had long had his suspicions that Petra murdered Danny Linton, but now there was no doubt about it. Bernard Lavoisier was virtually an eyewitness.

He was about to continue questioning for more details, when it occurred to him that Rod still hadn't arrived. Maybe he'd left a message. Remembering the lack of signal in 'Crocker's Corner', with the words, 'Just got to make a call', he stepped outside the pub.

The air was still summer-evening warm. As he moved towards the Midget, the mobile rang. It was Rod. Presumably, about to explain why he hadn't yet reached the Goat & Compasses.

'It's brilliant, Major!' The boy's voice from the phone

was squeaky with excitement. 'There are so many valuable paintings hidden behind the ordinary ones!'

Damn. He'd told Rod just to take the one piece of evidence and get the hell out of the house as quickly as possible.

'Because you said how good it was that I was doing things on my own initiative, so I thought I could do more things on my own initiative and provide more research for—'

His voice was interrupted by the offstage sound of a door opening. 'Who are you? Look, I didn't mean to—'

There was an ominous thump and the phone went dead.

Though Stunston Peveril was a very small village with every destination walkable, the Major leapt into the Midget with Nga Luong to drive to Noel Palgrave's house.

The front door was ajar. Switching on his phone light, he gingerly pushed his way in.

The beam inspected the walls of the hall. There was no sign of any packaged-up paintings.

More worryingly, there was no sign of Rod.

14

Another Break-In

'I have done everything you have asked of me,' asserted the Employee.

'Yes,' the Employer responded tetchily, 'but you have not done it all in the way I wanted it done.'

'I've got the results, haven't I?'

'At some cost. Because of your actions, at least one of my operations will have to be closed down.'

'You've got plenty of others.'

'That is not the point!' The tetchiness was now closer to anger. 'I do not like failure. In everything I attempt, I always succeed!'

'If it makes you feel better, you can blame me for the cock-up,' said the Employee, getting a bit tired of the constant criticism.

'I already do blame you. But that doesn't make any difference. You were acting on my instructions, so the failure reflects on me.'

'Except, because they are all undercover operations, no one is aware of your failure.'

'That is not the point!' the Employer repeated, this time in fury.

'Look, we've got them all here. Now we can deal with them.'

'We have not got them all here! The one who is missing is that troublemaker, Major Bricket.'

'Don't worry,' the Employee reassured with an evil smile. 'I'll put money on the fact that he's already on his way.'

Major Bricket was already on his way. Alone. He'd left Nga Luong to return to the Green Lotus. She had plans for what she was going to do the minute she got inside.

Before leaving for the Goat & Compasses earlier in the evening, the Major had gone down to his armoury to select a suitable weapon for the encounters that he was anticipating. He didn't have to think about it, instinctively unchaining his Heckler & Koch USP Compact, a favourite semi-automatic he'd owned for nearly twenty years. He had loaded it with the maximum thirteen rounds, which he thought would deal with most eventualities, and slipped it into his jacket pocket.

Also, while still at Highfield House, he had checked out the burglary maps which Nipper Wilkinson had drawn for Rod Enright all those years before. Endearingly, the printed exterior and interior plans had pencil notes scribbled on them, in what must have been the boy's slightly childish handwriting.

On one of the maps, he saw that Rod had written the name of the building featured. He had first written 'Highfield House', then crossed that out and replaced it with the words 'Highhouse Hall'.

Major Bricket remembered Rod talking about his confusion over the similarity between the two addresses.

Suddenly, as he drove the Midget out of Stunston

Peveril late that evening, the relevance of that mix-up came to him.

And it did explain a lot about the murder of Danny Linton.

The prisoners – for, in spite of their luxurious surroundings, there was no other way to describe them – looked at each other ruefully. They were hemmed in by priceless artworks and antiques in one of Highhouse Hall's many drawing rooms, but the doors were as firmly locked as they would have been in cells in Wormwood Scrubs. And they were in handcuffs.

Rod Enright was still a little woozy from the blow to the head he'd sustained in Noel Palgrave's house. His recollections of the journey from there to his current accommodation were imprecise. He had vague memories of travelling in a van and being manhandled by men in black uniforms.

'Surely they'll just let us go?' he suggested hopefully.

Piotr Jankowski's response was not encouraging. 'No chance of that,' he said in heavily accented English. 'My wife Petra does not forgive. We have been brought here because we have upset her plans. She has no sympathy for people who upset her plans. She will have her revenge on us.'

'What form,' asked Rod tentatively, 'will that revenge take?'

'That,' Piotr replied, 'is not a question it is good to ask.'

The boundaries of the Highhouse Hall estate were extensive. Major Bricket parked the Midget at the point indicated on Nipper Wilkinson's map. The perimeter fence was electrified and alarmed, except for this one gateway, through which maintenance vehicles came in and out. (The drivers were meant to reconnect the wiring when they used the entrance but, apparently, had got very lax in following the procedure every time.)

Fortunately, their laxity continued. The Major's opening the gate did not set anything off. He closed it, checked once more that the USP Compact was still in his jacket pocket. From the other one, he withdrew a slim torch with a very narrow beam and, pointing that down at his feet, advanced across the parkland towards Highhouse Hall. He made mental notes of which rooms had their lights on, already planning his route for when he was inside the building.

Back at the Goat & Compasses, the masculine comfort of 'Crocker's Corner' was ruffled by the arrival of an angry ring mistress in full performance kit.

'Dad,' said Camille, 'you should have stayed for the company march-round at the end!'

'Oh, for heaven's sake!' said her father.

'No, it's one of the basic rules of circus, one that you taught me. Wherever you are in the running order, however small a part you played, you must always appear in the company march-round.'

'Look, Camille, I only knew I was on the bill this afternoon.'

'That's not the point.'

The Great Pantherleo interceded on his partner's behalf. 'Camille, we were just so elated by how The Plastered Plasterers had gone down, we wanted to celebrate.' He raised his sparkling mineral water to demonstrate. 'And we realise that was very wrong, going against all the traditions of circus, but we have been out of the performing side for quite a while.'

His emollient pleading did soften the ring mistress's anger. A little bit, anyway. 'Well, don't do it again.'

'You mean there will be an "again"?' asked the lion-tamer.

'Of course there will,' Camille assured him. 'The Plastered Plasterers are booked for as long as Lavoisier's Circus remains in business.'

The double act looked at each other in delight, and then high-fived in a gleeful manner which belied their age.

'That's brilliant news!' said Crocker Fosbury.

'Brilliant!' said Derek, almost overlapping with his brother.

'Dad,' said Camille, 'what's happened to you?'

'Happened to me? What do you mean?'

'Since this afternoon you've been totally transformed. I haven't seen you like this since Mum died. What's made the sudden change?'

'Ah,' said her father. 'It's because Petra's gone.'

'Oh?' Camille looked perplexed.

'Now she's gone, I no longer feel my life is threatened. I can talk about things that I couldn't mention since I did the deal with her.'

'Deal? Dad, I don't know what you're talking about.'

'There's so much stuff I can tell you now, Cam.'

She couldn't think when her father had last used that affectionate abbreviation. 'Like what?' she asked.

'I can tell you who's been funding Lavoisier's Circus for the last few years.'

'Who?'

'Carkvale Stuke.' There was a silence. 'Have you heard of them?'

'Yes. Yes, I have.'

'A company set up by Petra – under her full name, Petra Jankowska.'

Camille Lavoisier didn't look convinced by this, but she made no comment.

'I can also tell you who killed Danny Linton!'

'Oh?' His daughter's grey eyes narrowed. 'Can you?'

At Highhouse Hall, in his study, furnished like a gentleman's club with a couple of Gainsboroughs and a Turner on the wall, Lord Piers Goodruff was sharing a bottle of 1982 Pétrus with Petra Jankowska. Needless to say, she wasn't wearing her black leather bikini. She looked good in a Sabina Bilenko cocktail dress.

The peer's mouth was twisted in an expression of reproof. 'We didn't want to pull the plugs on the Lavoisier's Circus operation so soon.'

'It was always limited returns,' Petra objected.

'Yeah, maybe. But a return's a return. We don't like putting the lid on any business that's still making a profit.'

'Look, I killed Danny Linton, as per instructions. And I planted the evidence in Massimo's caravan, as per instructions.'

Lord Goodruff shook his head impatiently, as if he'd either never heard of – or else had no interest in – the details of the murder. 'We're careful where we invest. An unsuccessful investment is bad for our image.'

'Oh, come on,' said Petra. 'You've got enough money.'

The peer reacted vigorously. She was challenging one of the guiding principles of his life. 'You can *never* have enough money!'

'OK. Still,' Petra argued, 'the Lavoisier's Circus project is going to have to be disbanded, anyway.'

'Why? People still want drugs – and we've found the perfect way to distribute them round the country.'

'Yes, but the rate at which the circus is losing its acts means it's going to struggle to survive, anyway. Massimo will soon be in the nick.'

'You don't think there's any danger of someone proving his innocence?'

'No chance. The police have got what they wanted. A perpetrator with lots of evidence that he did it. They're very happy, so there's no way they're going to poke a stick back into that particular hornets' nest.'

'OK.' He didn't sound totally reassured.

'Then, after what's happened, there's no way I can go back to Lavoisier's. And that conniving bastard Piotr won't be going back either.'

'Well, we've got him locked up here, haven't we?' said Goodruff with satisfaction. 'With the boy.'

'So, the paintings will soon be on their way to the Crown Prince of Qajjiah . . . which must mean that operation's also finished now?'

'Yes. Not finished in quite the way we'd hoped, but finished. The money's as good as in our account.'

'So, the question remains . . .' said Petra. 'What do we do with the two of them?'

'Our prisoners?'

'Yes.'

'They still have to be punished.'

'Piers, are you still thinking of punishing them in the way you suggested?'

'Oh yes.' He grinned. 'I've always liked mixing a bit of showbiz into my revenges.'

The instructions on Nipper Wilkinson's map were very clear. And, as in the break-in to Noel Palgrave's house, entering the building involved knowing a code to access a hidden key. How Nipper had obtained that code, Major Bricket had no idea. He just hoped it hadn't been changed since the map was created.

And he had to be more cautious than Rod had been. Noel Palgrave's house was assumed to be unoccupied. Whereas it was well known that Highhouse Hall had a large staff of servants.

The map directed him to the back right-hand side of the building, a part of the mansion that housed the kitchens and other servants' areas. Clearly marked was a rectangle against the back wall, with the words 'coal chute' scribbled in.

The metal doors were set in a brick extension, which made them look as if they were leaning at a low angle against the main house. Matching metal rings on the edges were secured with a rustproof marine padlock. Robust – nobody was going to saw through that in a hurry.

Major Bricket turned the padlock upwards to reveal the numbers display. He focused his torch beam and turned the cogs until they lined up the code that was written on Nipper's map. '2081'.

It hadn't been changed. He slipped the opened padlock out of the rings and lifted back one door. His torch showed that, though its cleanliness suggested it hadn't been used recently for its original purpose, the chute was still a cement slope down to the cellar.

He eased himself down, then reached up to close the open door. No need to advertise his presence to any security guard who might be passing outside.

Major Bricket was inside Highhouse Hall.

Rod and Piotr had not encountered Murkish before, but his uniform identified him as the Highhouse Hall butler. Accompanied by two burly men in black, he had opened the door to the drawing room where the prisoners were being held.

'Lord Goodruff wants them in the Library,' said Murkish.

In their handcuffed state, there was no point in trying to resist. Meekly, the prisoners followed the men in black. Murkish did not accompany them. He had other duties inside Highhouse Hall.

Camille Lavoisier sped through the Suffolk countryside. She had a feeling that events were moving towards a climax. The news of who had killed Danny Linton was out. So was the news of who'd been funding Lavoisier's Circus.

The trouble was that, with the spread of that knowledge would come a lot of inevitable knock-on effects. Some of which could be good, from her point of view, some bad.

It was down to her to ensure that they were good.

In other circumstances, Major Bricket might have paused to have a look at the array of bottles in the wine cellar.

The few labels he could see promised great riches. But he did not stop. He had other priorities. And he was a whisky man, after all.

As he mounted the stairs, the Major became extra-vigilant. There had not been much danger of encountering anyone in the cellars. The same was not true in the rest of the house.

Before he opened the door that led there, he checked his bearings on Nipper's map of the interior.

The scene that greeted Rod and Piotr in the Library was not encouraging. The wheel that Petra and Piotr used in their act was set up in front of the tall windows.

Lord Goodruff sat in another Louis Quinze chair, in a state of gleeful anticipation. On a small table which had also once graced Versailles, Petra had laid out the full set of twelve knives which she and her husband had used in their act.

Half a dozen impassive black-clad servants stood around the edges of the room.

Ominously, on top of the priceless Savonnerie carpet on which the knife-throwers' wheel would have rested, was plastic sheeting. Just like that laid down in anticipation of slapstick scenes. But neither of the prisoners thought it had been put there to keep off water or whitewash.

'We thought it would be rather fun,' announced Lord Goodruff to the prisoners, 'if we did your punishment like a circus act.'

Silence.

'Piotr, I gather from Petra that, at Lavoisier's Circus, you have been "Facing Death Daily from the Razor-Sharp Knives!" Except, she tells me, usually you've been the one throwing the knives at her. But, in these egalitarian times, is that really fair? Would the #MeToo cohort be happy about that? How's about we try it with you on the wheel and Petra with the knives?'

Husband and wife had not exchanged a look since Piotr had been brought into the room. Now, with some bravado, he replied, 'That suit me fine. Petra is at least as skilled with the knives as I am.'

'Isn't that great?' said Lord Goodruff.

'She will be able to miss my body with the knives just as well as I miss hers.'

'Good, good.' An Australian chuckle. 'That is, of course, if she wants to miss.'

'We will find out about that,' said Piotr, still not looking at his potential nemesis. 'Go on then, strap me up there!'

'Oh yes, we will. Shortly. But not quite yet. I'd like to see evidence of your knife skills first.' Suddenly, Lord Goodruff snapped at his servants, 'Strap the boy up!'

As two of them moved forward to obey the command, Piotr objected, 'No, that is not fair. The boy's life will be in danger.'

'Surely that's up to you, and your skills as a thrower.'

'No, it is more than that. Petra and I worked on the act for years before we showed it to the public. What the audience see is man throwing knives at completely passive woman. But that is not it. Woman as much a part of act as man. She make very small movements. She control speed of wheel. There is a kind of brake she operates with her foot. If you put on the wheel someone who does not know the tricks, they will die!'

Lord Goodruff shrugged. 'Well, that's just a risk we'll

have to take, isn't it?'

Piotr looked in desperation as Rod was splayed out on the wooden wheel and leather thongs were strapped around his wrists and ankles. Bravely, the boy let out no cries of protest.

Piotr appealed desperately to his wife. 'Petra, we must stop them doing this! The boy will die!'

She did not even look at him.

Fortunately, Major Bricket's training meant he was skilled at moving unseen through occupied buildings. Inside Highhouse Hall, he clocked the approach of black-clad servants going about their duties and hid in a good few doorways or behind curtains as he drew near to the main reception rooms.

There was no one about as he got close to the hidden door. It had been wallpapered over, but not in such a way as to stop it from opening. As the article in *Suffolk's Historic Homes* had suggested, the feature had been preserved as an oddity to show to private visitors.

Major Bricket slid his fingers down the wallpapered edge and opened the door. Then, removing the USP Compact from his pocket, he slipped inside the Priest Hole.

'Spin the wheel!' Lord Goodruff shouted the order.

Rod, petrified but still silent, was spreadeagled across the wheel, as one of the black-clad servants followed his employer's command. In its new environment, the wheel spun as easily as it ever had in the ring of Lavoisier's Circus.

'Start throwing the knives!' came the next order.

Frozen to the spot, Piotr Jankowski did nothing.

Then his wife's voice, silky but compelling, repeated the command. 'Piotr, start throwing the knives!'

As if hypnotised – perhaps he was incapable of crossing his wife in anything – he raised his hand to throw the first knife.

Afterwards, no one could positively state that they saw Major Bricket's actual entrance from the other door of the Priest Hole. But suddenly he was in the Library.

And suddenly, Lord Goodruff found he had the barrel of a Heckler & Koch USP Compact nestling under his chin.

'Don't any of you make a move!' said the Major in a voice that had wielded authority in many international crises. 'I really will not hesitate to shoot.'

They believed him. Nobody moved.

'Because there are quite a number of crimes you're guilty of, aren't there, Goodruff?'

The peer of the realm said nothing. The wattles below his jaw trembled.

'Where shall we start? God knows what illegal proceedings you were involved in in Australia before you arrived here, but you certainly had sufficient funds to buy your way into British society. And a lot of your businesses, at least on the surface, were legitimate – the newspapers, television companies, hotels, football clubs, your investment in Qajjiah Airlines. Those didn't break any laws – at least no more than such enterprises owned by billionaires might be expected to.

'But that wasn't enough for you, was it? You were greedy for more money, more of everything. And the easiest way of achieving that was by involvement in major crime. You became a kind of bent venture capitalist, bankrolling crooks and gangs – and creaming off a nice percentage of your profits.'

Lord Goodruff finally managed to speak. 'You can't prove any of this.'

'I'm sorry to disappoint you,' said the Major coolly, 'but I'm afraid I can. Bernard Lavoisier is prepared to talk about the drugs dealership you set up through his circus. To save their own skins, Noel Palgrave and Nipper Wilkinson will be more than ready to admit to their part in the art theft deal with the Crown Prince of Qajjiah. I'm sure, once the investigation into your business affairs starts, Goodruff, a lot more skeletons will come rattling out of cupboards.

'And then, of course, there's the matter of Danny Linton's murder.'

'I didn't do it!' said the noble peer. 'I wasn't involved at all.'

'No, you didn't pull the trigger. Petra did that. And, incidentally, Petra,' the Major turned to the owner of the name, 'I suggest you put down that knife you've just picked up or I really will shoot your boss.'

For a moment, the thought crossed the woman's mind that that might not be such a bad idea. But consideration of the consequences such an action could trigger persuaded her to replace the knife on the table.

'And move over to by the wheel!' the Major barked. Petra did as instructed.

Major Bricket continued, 'As I say, Petra killed Danny Linton.'

'You have no proof!' Petra asserted.

'Bernard Lavoisier saw you carting the body out of your caravan.'

'He couldn't be certain it was a body. It could have been—'

'It could have been many things. But, in fact, it was a body. Danny Linton's body. Whom you had just shot. And there was a witness to the actual murder.'

'No, there wasn't! I was alone when—'

'No, you weren't,' the Major interrupted smoothly. He turned to the woman's husband. 'Piotr, you were in the caravan when Petra shot Danny, weren't you?'

'Yes, I was.' The man's voice was thick with emotion.

'And would you be prepared to stand up in court and say that?'

There was a long silence. The knife-thrower tried to avoid the fiery eyes that his wife was focusing on him. Then – possibly emboldened by the fact that he was unlikely to leave the Library alive, anyway – he said firmly, 'Yes. Yes, I would.'

Major Bricket was on a roll now. 'And I think, while we're on the subject of Danny Linton's murder, we should mention the important detail you got wrong, Petra.'

'I don't know what you mean.'

'Oh, you do. You very definitely do. One part of the instructions you were given you misunderstood – or possibly misheard. You left the body in the garage of my place, Highfield House. Reasonable mistake to make for someone unfamiliar with the area. Quite a lot of locals get it wrong.' He appealed to the young man still trapped to the wheel. 'You used to get confused about it, didn't you, Rod? The instructions you received, Petra, told you to leave the body, not in the garage of Highfield House, but in the garage of Highhouse Hall!

'And, once one realises that, a whole lot of other

anomalies are explained. That kind of killing in criminal circles is usually done as a warning to the person on whose property the corpse is found. It's a calling card, like the famous Mafia horse's head. It's saying, "Watch your step – or you'll be next!" And the fact that the body was wearing a clown suit also has some relevance to the intended target. But I couldn't think of a reason why anyone might be sending those messages to *me*.

'But if the corpse in the clown suit had been found in the garage here, at Highhouse Hall ... well, that opens up a whole new range of possibilities, doesn't it? So, who was the message being sent to?

'You might think the gentleman into whose neck my semi-automatic pistol is currently nuzzling is the obvious target. But that conclusion is rather hard to fit with the certain facts which we know to be true. If, as I'm sure we have all been assuming, Lord Goodruff is the mastermind behind all of these criminal enterprises, why would he send such a dramatic warning message to *himself*?

'So, this makes me think, perhaps we've all been barking up the wrong tree. Our assumption that Goodruff is the ultimate boss may be false. Maybe the ultimate boss is the one who wanted Goodruff to understand the meaning of a corpse in a clown suit found in his garage here at Highhouse Hall.'

There was a moment of stunned silence.

Now, it is a well-known fact in fiction that butlers make no sound when they move. There are plenty of examples from the works of P. G. Wodehouse of Jeeves simply manifesting himself at Bertie Wooster's side. Those are moments of pure joy. What happened next in the Highhouse Hall Library was more sinister.

Murkish had suddenly manifested himself behind Major Bricket's back. How he'd entered didn't matter. He was there. And the blow he struck to Major Bricket's arm sent the USP Compact flying from its owner's hand.

The tables were very definitely turned. Lord Goodruff was now holding Major Bricket's gun and, from somewhere, Murkish had produced his own semi-automatic pistol.

'Now order has been restored,' said Goodruff, 'I think we'll go back to where we were before we were so rudely interrupted. As I recall, we were about to punish some malefactors.'

'Yes,' said Petra eagerly. 'By throwing knives at the boy on the wheel.'

'And I can see no reason why we should change our plans,' said the peer.

'I think we should have an expert to do the job.' Petra's voice was venomously silky. 'Piotr, you claim to be one of the best knife-throwers in Europe.'

'Yes, I am, but not with a target who has never practised the routine.'

'Well, that's the target you've got today,' said his wife, on a note of triumph. 'Not me, I'm afraid . . . because I'll be the one who's turning the wheel!'

Piotr went pale. 'But the wheel speed has to be precisely regulated. If it's not, something bad can happen.'

'I am well aware of that. I am also well aware of my ability to change the speed of the wheel whenever I feel like it.'

The cruelty of the fate that awaited him was not lost on Rod. But he still made no sound. No weeping, no pleading. Major Bricket's mind, which was bursting with potential escape plans, had room to appreciate such stoicism.

'Twelve knives. I've been told that is what you usually use in your act. Am I right?' asked Goodruff.

'You are,' Petra replied.

'But less,' Piotr beseeched them. 'Less.'

'Twelve,' said his implacable wife, as she came towards him with the blindfold. She checked it before putting it on him.

'No, not that way round!' cried Piotr. 'It will be murder!'

'That way round,' Petra confirmed. Then she turned him round three times to disorient him and moved away.

'So,' she said, 'the rules are: You have to throw all twelve knives. If any of them miss the wheel or fall out, they have to be thrown again. Agreed, Piers?'

'Agreed.'

'Agreed, Murkish?'

'Agreed.'

'Right,' said Petra. 'I am about to turn the wheel. Piotr, allow the usual thirty seconds for the wheel to get up to speed, then throw the first knife.'

'And if I do not?'

'Then,' said Lord Goodruff,' we'll find another way to kill the boy.'

'And, after I've thrown all twelve,' Piotr pleaded, 'you let boy go – no?'

'We might do that,' Lord Goodruff replied. 'We'll see how we feel.'

'Rod,' said the knife-thrower. They'd exchanged names when first imprisoned together. 'Rod, say something, so I know exactly where you are.'

'Good luck!' came the plucky response.

With ferocious concentration, the knife-thrower orientated himself and listened to the slight hissing of the wheel turning. He had worked with it so long that his ear was attuned to the slightest change of pitch.

'Wheel up to speed!' shouted Petra. 'Throw the first knife!'

Major Bricket could hardly watch. He'd never felt closer to the boy. He must protect him. For his mother Sylvia's sake.

The first knife's point thudded into the wheel, on the edge, a good six inches away from Rod's right arm. The second was closer, this time to his left arm.

Up until then, Petra, as ever turning the wheel clockwise, had kept the speed steady. Now, she started playing games, suddenly speeding up, then almost slowing to a standstill.

Still, the knives flew. Eight more thudded into the wood around the outline of Rod Enright's body. The eleventh crashed home high up between the boy's legs. That prompted a little whimper, but the blade had not breached his skin.

Then, for the last throw, Petra went against all the rules of knife-throwing. She stopped the wheel and immediately made it turn anticlockwise.

The tension around Piotr's mouth was almost bursting the skin, as he threw the twelfth knife. It thumped into the wood just above Rod's head. It even cut off a bit of his hair.

Piotr's whole body slumped with relief.

'Jolly good show! Well played, that man,' said Major Bricket, for all the world as if he was applauding an MCC century at Lord's. 'All right. He's had his punishment. Let the boy go!'

'Oh, no,' said Petra. 'The punishment isn't complete yet. Shall we try the variation we talked about, Piers?'

'Bonzer idea!' said the noble lord.

Without even looking at him, Petra ripped the blindfold off her husband's face. And held it out towards Major Bricket. 'Your turn now.'

'And, if you don't do it, we might be tempted to shoot you,' said Goodruff. 'Isn't that right, Murkish?'

'Yes, milord,' said the butler, in a manner that was anything but subservient.

Major Bricket was, as ever, completely rational. He assessed the situation. His instinct was not to throw the knives. In such circumstances, he always evaluated the relative importance of individual lives. And the boy's life was much more important than his own. While he was working, the Major had already had more experiences than fill many other people's lifetimes. Rod Enright was just embarking on what, the Major hoped, would be an equally exciting journey.

On the other hand ... If he allowed himself to be shot now, Major Bricket would have no opportunity of saving the boy from his current predicament. And, because of the bond he'd shared with Rod's mother Sylvia, he regarded it as his mission in life to protect the boy.

He had worked with knives before. Used them – or at least used dummy ones – in hand-to-hand combat training. On occasions, at moments of jeopardy in foreign climes, he had used ones that weren't dummies. If an enemy had come at him wielding a dagger, there was a pretty reasonable chance the Major could have bested him.

But, blindfolded, to throw knives at someone tied to a moving wheel without causing injury ... that was a different skill altogether.

He looked around the Library, in the hope of seeing someone who might help him, but he knew it was hopeless. The only two people rooting for him were Rod and Piotr. One was strapped to the wheel, the other had been re-handcuffed and was now held between two of Goodruff's black-suited thugs.

'Don't play for time!' came the peremptory shout from Petra. 'Throw the first knife!'

'And don't forget,' Lord Goodruff added, 'knives that don't stay in the wheel have to be thrown again.'

'Can I do what Piotr did? Ask Rod to say something so I can at least be facing in the right direction?'

Without waiting for permission, the boy cried out, 'Good luck!'

Well, he thought to himself, it had worked the last time.

Major Bricket didn't have the same confidence in history repeating itself. He said a brief mental prayer to the God he didn't believe in, then steadied himself into a throwing stance, grasped the sharp end of the first knife and sent it spinning across the room.

A satisfying thud of metal embedding itself into wood, and no howl of pain. The luck had held for one knife. What were the chances of it holding for another cleven?

Slim, thought the Major, as he felt across the table and picked up the second murderous weapon. He felt frustrated. He had come so close to settling the case. He felt confident he now knew who the ultimate controller of the operations was, the one whose criminal instructions all the others followed. But it currently looked as if he'd be frustrated in his attempts to bring the villain to justice.

He held the sharp end of the knife tight and raised his arm once again into the throwing position.

But, before it was despatched on its lethal journey, he heard a commotion behind him. Tearing off the blindfold, he saw the main doors to the Library being opened by servants, to admit, still resplendent in her ring mistress outfit, Camille Lavoisier.

The Employer and the Employee exchanged looks.

15

Confrontations in the Library

Major Bricket took the momentary confusion as an opportunity to snatch back his USP Compact from Goodruff. Murkish, he noticed, put away his gun. For some reason, the butler didn't want the new arrival to see any signs of criminality in the Library (though it might be hard for her not to notice a young man strapped to a wooden wheel).

Camille Lavoisier, however, appeared not to see him. Her grey eyes scanned the room to locate the one person in the Library she was interested in. She strode across the floor to confront Petra. 'I have many bones to pick with you,' she announced.

'I don't think so,' the woman responded. 'I have never let you down. I have always followed your instructions to the letter.'

'That is not what I'm talking about!' shouted the furious ring mistress. 'I can never forgive you for the way you treated my father.'

'Your father's a drunken old fool. If I wasn't taking advantage of him, someone else would be.'

'But the way you blackmailed him through your Carkvale Stuke set-up ... The way you got Lavoisier's

Circus involved in drug dealing. I can never forgive you for those things!'

'I think,' Major Bricket interposed, 'you're rather barking up the wrong tree here, Camille.'

'What do you mean?'

'Do you really believe that Petra Jankowska, skilled in being part of a world-class knife-throwing act, but with absolutely zero knowledge of the business world, could possibly set up a company with—'

'But she inherited the money from a relative in Poland and—'

'Arrant cobblers, Camille,' said the Major firmly. 'The money that appeared to have rescued Lavoisier's Circus certainly came from the proprietor of Carkvale Stuke. As did the conditions that came with that money. But it wasn't Petra laying down the law. She was merely a mouthpiece for the real owner of Carkvale Stuke. Isn't that true, Petra?'

She denied the allegation hotly, but with so little conviction that she wasn't even convincing herself.

'My research team,' Major Bricket went on grandly, 'has found out a lot about Carkvale Stuke. A lot of dirt, I'm afraid. Providing funding for some of the world's biggest criminal operators. When it's all made public, the people behind it are going to go down for very long sentences.' He turned to face his quarry. 'Aren't you, Lord Goodruff?'

The peer remained calm. 'If your research team think I own Carkvale Stuke, they're definitely not a very good research team. I may have put money into Carkvale Stuke, that's certainly true. When my brokers tell me about some company that's cleaning up, I tend to follow their advice and invest. Rather large amounts. I doubt if you've ever had much money to invest. Have you, Major?'

He did not bother responding to this basic rudeness. Instead, he said sedately, 'I haven't suggested that you do own Carkvale Stuke, Lord Goodruff. All I'm saying is that you're sufficiently involved in the company for the public revelation of what's been going on to end your career.'

The Australian looked thoughtful. 'Why're you involved in this, Major? What are you getting out of it?'

'The satisfaction of seeing justice done.'

'Oh yes. That's sounds very admirable, doesn't it? Very British. Old School Tie and all that garbage. But what are you getting out of it . . . financially?'

'I have a very adequate pension, thank you, Lord Goodruff,' said Major Bricket.

'Yes, but we could all do with a bit *more* . . . couldn't we?' came the wheedling response.

'That is where you are wrong, Goodruff. You mustn't judge everyone by your own standards. And, if you were about to offer me some well-paid sinecure in one of your companies – or just a lot of good, old-fashioned money . . . to make me change my principles, I'm afraid you're talking to the wrong person. I don't get my kicks from owning things . . . or people. But I will derive enormous pleasure from the knowledge that you are behind bars.'

When the Australian next spoke, his tone had changed. He was now petulant – and even a bit frightened. 'You can't blame me for any of it! The businesses in which I made my name – and my fortune – were all legitimate. Then I kind of got mixed up with someone who was a bad influence and they introduced me to all these other ways of making money and I . . .' He looked paranoid now. 'Do you want me to tell you who it is?'

'Or,' asked the Major, 'shall I tell you who it is?'

He looked round the room. Camille Lavoisier's beautiful face was as impassive as ever. No one would ever know what went on inside her magnificent brain.

'The mastermind behind all these criminal enterprises,' said Major Bricket, 'is Ludwig Murkish.'

The butler's pistol was already back in his hand.

'Under cover of his work, mixing with the world's rich and famous,' the Major went on, 'he has built up an international crime network. Carkvale Stuke is just one of many financial engines he has organised all over the world. So, Petra, when you are arrested for the murder of Danny Linton – as you undoubtedly will be – you could try the old "only following orders" defence. You could pin the blame on the man who gave you the instructions to kill – Ludwig Murkish!'

The butler grinned and spoke in his customary measured tones. 'You are, of course, right, Major Bricket. Mine is the ideal cover for a criminal mastermind. Working for the rich and famous, one very soon realises how stupid they are with money – and how readily they will agree to any plan which is going to make them more of the stuff. Their consciences are pleasingly flexible. They can quickly forget that their new sources of income are, in fact, criminal operations.

'And when they do realise it, they are in far too deep to get out. I wouldn't wish to use the word blackmail, but I do always have enough evidence of their wrongdoing to stop them from exposing me to the police.

'Lord Goodruff is the perfect example – too greedy to resist getting involved in schemes I set up for him. And, at bottom, rather a stupid man. In other words, an ideal pawn in my master plan.'

Major Bricket glanced across at the Australian, who looked frankly terrified. It was a measure of how much control the butler had over him, as Murkish continued, 'But, occasionally, these wealthy worms will turn, start to think that they are in charge rather than me. In the case of Lord Goodruff, he did rather more than that. He had the temerity to describe butlers as "clowns". I couldn't let him get away with that. He needed a warning.

'Danny Linton was already a thorn in my side. He'd been helping himself to the profits from the Lavoisier's Circus drug-dealing business. He needed to be punished. And I could kill two birds with one stone – or one bullet, as it turned out. I could get rid of a low-ranking enemy – and I could send a strong warning to Lord Goodruff of the dangers of describing butlers as "clowns" in the *Daily Mail*.'

Major Bricket got it. Like most criminal masterminds, Ludwig Murkish had a very thin skin. In fact, he was paranoid. He had misinterpreted Lord Goodruff's interview (the one Nga Luong had found and photocopied) describing the whole British Establishment as 'clowns'. Major Bricket recalled Goodruff's words. 'The people who have got to the top from inherited wealth – they're just a bunch of clowns. I have contempt for their titles, their stately homes, their art collections, their shooting parties, their MCC memberships, their gentlemen's clubs, their air of superiority, their butlers. They're all clowns.'

He had read that as an insult to butlers, or to one butler in particular – Ludwig Murkish.

'And,' the villain continued, 'my plan would have worked, but for the crass stupidity of the operative who I instructed to commit the crime – and her planting the body in its clown suit *in the wrong garage!*'

'How dare you call me stupid!' Petra Jankowska's face seethed with fury. 'I thought I was working on the instructions of an aristocrat.' She picked up one of the throwing knives. 'But to discover that I was obeying a mere servant! I will kill you!'

She rushed at Murkish with the knife. Major Bricket threw his body forward to intercept her. Murkish raised his gun.

And at that moment, the main doors to the Library burst open, to reveal Detective Inspector Pritchett with a back-up of armed officers in uniform. Right at the back of the group stood Nga Luong, who, having heard in the Goat & Compasses that Petra had murdered Danny Linton, had done the right thing – and summoned the proper authorities.

The Inspector announced, 'I have come here to arrest someone.' He looked around the room to assess who his quarry might be.

What happened next happened very quickly. Murkish, gun still in hand, rushed at the French windows, smashed through them and disappeared into the garden.

Petra, waving her throwing knife, followed him, shouting imprecations in Polish.

Moments later, car sounds were heard. Murkish had taken one of the Bentleys from the garage (the garage where he had intended Danny Linton's body should be found as a warning to Lord Goodruff). And Petra, in her gleaming electric BMW, had driven off in hot pursuit.

The Employee was chasing the Employer.

Detective Inspector Pritchett was still not sure who he was meant to be arresting. Major Bricket whispered a word in his ear, and the 'proper authorities' put handcuffs on Lord Goodruff.

The relief of tension was palpable. The black-clad servants, with their two major persecutors removed, relaxed visibly. They started to gossip and joke together.

Major Bricket chatted to Camille Lavoisier about the rejuvenation that reviving The Plastered Plasterers act seemed to have wrought in her father.

But then he was distracted by rather a pathetic voice. It was Rod Enright asking, 'Could someone get me off this thing, please?'

16

Stunston Peveril Settles Back Down Again

Though the mastermind behind all the criminal activities had escaped, investigations into the affairs of Lord Piers Goodruff found him knee-deep in everything. The Lavoisier's Circus drug dealing and the scam of selling stolen paintings to the Crown Prince of Qajjiah were just two of the many illegal operations from which he was profiting through Carkvale Stuke, the company owned by Ludwig Murkish.

The British police – who had never liked him, anyway – had a field day with Lord Goodruff. Other authorities, like the taxman, became involved, and all the legitimate Goodruff businesses were brought down with the illegal ones. He was ruined, both financially and socially. His upmarket friends – who had never liked him, anyway – all shunned his company. The many mistresses of the colour-coded bedrooms – who had never liked him, anyway – stopped answering his calls. Everywhere, he was *persona non grata*.

Since he'd made no friends on the way up, there were none to commiserate with him on the way down.

Though, bizarrely, because that's the way the law

works in England, he retained his title and his seat in the House of Lords.

All the paintings that had been stolen from Fincham Abbey were taken back there and replaced in their frames. Viscount and Viscountess Wintle did not make much fuss about their return. After all, they'd never noticed they were missing.

But that detail allowed Perpetua finally to persuade her husband that they could sell a few of the paintings. Having admitted to being unaware of their absence, he couldn't really argue. And the proceeds of the sales did allow them to employ more staff and live in greater comfort at Fincham Abbey. With a butler. Not a villain like Murkish. They engaged a venerably respectful character whose nostalgia for the feudal system was almost stronger than the Viscount's.

Noel Palgrave and Nipper Wilkinson were charged over their involvement in the theft of the paintings, and both served time in prison. Eva Wilkinson moved away from the village as soon as her husband was sentenced, taking the two dogs with her. What the two malefactors did when they came out, nobody knew. Or cared much. After all, they were no longer Stunston Peveril people.

The Viscount and Viscountess continued doddering on. One effect that their recent experience had was for the house insurance to be moved from the category of 'men's work' to that of 'women's work'. Like more or less everything else in Fincham Abbey. So, the paintings were protected from further skulduggery.

And Gregory focused on his one remaining duty. He

started planning what costume he might wear for the next year's costume ball. He rather fancied something piratical and began investigating where one went to get a wooden leg.

Meanwhile, he continued to moan about the way everything in Britain had 'gone to hell in a handcart'.

And Perpetua continued to exercise the skill she had perfected of making sympathetic noises to her husband without listening.

One thing the Viscount did say, as soon as Lavoisier's Circus had struck the Big Top and left Stunston Peveril, was: 'All I hope, Perpetua my dear, is that we never again allow circus folk onto Ratchetts Common.'

The Viscountess agreed that that was an excellent idea but was still determined to invite them the next year.

As it turned out, Viscount Wintle got his wish. Lavoisier's Circus did not survive after its visit to Stunston Peveril. Partly, that was due to loss of personnel. Obviously, Petra and Piotr were no longer on the bill.

And Massive Mazzini who was, needless to say, released when the news about Petra Jankowska's culpability emerged, didn't fancy rejoining the circus, anyway. Following his interest in the faith, he volunteered to work at a Buddhist temple in Godalming, where his strength was greatly appreciated for heavy lifting in the garden.

Soon, his deeper reading into such mysteries as the Eightfold Path and the Four Noble Truths led to him training to become a Buddhist monk.

The ending of the circus which had been Bernard Lavoisier's life might have depressed him and got him drinking even more. But it didn't work out that way, because of the success of The Plastered Plasterers.

Their last two performances, in Stunston Peveril, on the Saturday, had been triumphs.

By good fortune, a theatrical agent, who had a Suffolk cottage as a weekend retreat from his busy London life, saw the final show. And also saw potential in the act.

It was the appeal of the 'traditional', the same thing that made people with enough money grind their own corn and hang eel traps on their walls. The agent marketed the double act rather in the way that Ken Dodd had been sold in his later years. 'See this one-off phenomenon *live*, while the possibility to do so is still there!'

The Plastered Plasterers got spots on television shows and panel games. They were interviewed at length in *Saga Magazine*. And their fame was assured when their agent secured them a spot on the Royal Variety Show.

Bernard Lavoisier and Dr Hubert Devizes (he didn't call himself 'The Great Pantherleo' so much now) were in seventh heaven. Bernard, with a career to give his life a focus – and a career that involved climbing up wobbly ladders – stopped having any alcohol until after he'd done the show. And less then.

Camille Lavoisier wasn't too sad to see the circus go, either. She took a degree in Economics and Management at the LSE and soon developed a thriving career in the City as a venture capitalist. And she was very careful to ensure that the companies she invested in had no connection to crime.

*

Detective Inspector Pritchett continued his route up the police promotion ladder with great success. Thanks to secret briefings from Major Bricket, he was able to announce to the waiting press who had killed Danny Linton. And, though the suspect was still at large, he was confident she would soon be arrested, 'thanks to the efficiency of the British Police Force'.

In due time, Pritchett was promoted to Chief Inspector, unconsciously playing on the fact that nobody who met him could believe that he was really like the image of bumbling local bobby that he presented to the world. They were, of course, wrong. But those who overestimated his talents were in good company. Even someone as astute as Major Bricket had initially fallen into the same error.

No, with Detective Inspector Pritchett, what you saw was what you got. But that didn't prevent him from having a glittering career in the police force.

As it turned out, his hope that Petra would soon be caught 'thanks to the efficiency of the British Police Force' was not realised. She and Murkish had fled abroad, to involve themselves, no doubt, in more criminal activities.

But they hadn't fled together. Petra was still in pursuit of the man she felt had betrayed her by making her obey 'a servant'. Armed with her knives, she continued to search for him.

In the view of her former husband, Piotr, she would find him. Her determination was terrifying. And, when Petra did find him, Piotr didn't give much for Ludwig Murkish's chances.

*

Piotr Jankowski found himself at something of a loose end after Lavoisier's Circus closed. Well, before that, actually. There's never much work around for one half of a knife-throwing act.

But he did know about knives. So, he enrolled in a butchery course at a college in Norwich. And on the course he met a young woman who was a highly skilled cook. They got together and, after a few years, combined their skills to open a restaurant, not far from Stunston Peveril. Its Polish specials, *pierogi*, *placki* and *blinis*, are highly praised in the area.

The villagers of Stunston Peveril, it goes without saying, had views on the aftermath of Danny Linton's murder. And even more on the downfall of Lord Piers Goodruff.

In the Gingham Tea Shop, Elvira Finchcombe, untroubled by political correctness, said it was no surprise, because all Australians were descended from convicts.

Rhona in Cosy Collectibles, as usual, blamed illegal immigrants. By her reckoning, Lord Goodruff must have been an illegal immigrant from Australia.

In the view of Lena who cleaned at the vicarage, Lord Goodruff's mind had been taken over by the charismatic leader of a demonic cult. (Which, actually, wasn't a bad description of Ludwig Murkish.)

While Dierdre in the Post Office said that excavations Lord Goodruff had authorised at Highhouse Hall had upset some more Knights Templar.

In 'Crocker's Corner', Crocker still reckoned that everything that happened had something to do with aliens.

His brother Derek, in a rare moment of disagreement, expressed the opinion that some things didn't.

Soon after the departure of Lavoisier's Circus, Major Bricket went abroad for a while. On his return, going into the Gingham Tea Shop for a coffee, he found himself dragooned into sharing a table with Venetia Clothbury and Mollie Greenford.

'I gather you've been away,' said Venetia to all the café's customers (and, through its open windows, to passers-by in the streets nearby).

'Yes.'

'Where to?'

'Egypt.'

'Oh,' said Mollie Greenford. 'That sounds a horrible place to be. Did you read that about the hostage crisis in that school in Cairo?'

'I wouldn't know about that,' said the Major. 'Try to keep away from newspapers while I'm away.'

'Well, the kids did all get out,' said Mollie, 'thanks to the hostage negotiators. But it was touch and go for a while.'

'Oh dear. Anyway, I was nowhere near Cairo.'

'What were you doing out there?' demanded Venetia, never one to duck the direct question.

'Oh, I was studying church architecture,' said the Major.

'Erm ...' Mollie Greenford tentatively pointed out. 'Isn't Egypt a Muslim country? I didn't think there were many churches there.'

'No, you're absolutely right,' said the Major. 'But my interest does extend to mosque architecture.'

'Oh,' said Venetia Clothbury.

'Ah,' said Mollie Greenford.

'Do you know,' bellowed Venetia, 'the Village Committee is organising a talk tonight. On the subject: "What is the Right Frequency for the Recycling Bin Collections?"'

'Oh?'

'Are you planning to be there, Major?'

'See how things go,' he said.

In fact, he had forgotten that, however riveting the talk might have been, he did have another commitment that evening. A meal at Highfield House, with Rod and with Nga Luong who, obviously, would be cooking.

It was much more relaxed than their previous dinner. In a strange way, Rod's unpleasant experiences at Highhouse Hall seemed to have given him more confidence. Made him grow up a bit. And he'd got to know the other two better than he had at the first dinner.

Belgian beer was once again provided. The older two clinked their whisky glasses before Nga went through to the kitchen, from which exotic and tantalising smells emanated. In there, of course, she was using her dedicated Highfield House set of cooking equipment.

'Rod', said the Major, 'I've been looking at some courses that might suit you.'

'"Courses"?' came the contemptuous echo. 'You know I was always crap at schoolwork. "Not university material" – that's what the headmaster said to me.'

'I'm not talking about academic courses,' the Major reassured him. 'I meant things like rifle training and martial arts.'

'Ah.' The boy's brow cleared. 'I think I might like that.'

'I'll show you some stuff I've checked out online.'

They were interrupted by the welcome entrance of Nga, bearing their starters. The range included lotus root and shrimp salad, cellophane noodles with crabmeat, and vegetable tempura. To go with the last, there was a sweet soy dipping sauce, but that was only one of many small sauce dishes on the table. And, in case the display of goodies appeared too meagre, there was also a more substantial tamarind catfish soup.

Not much talking was done while the three of them luxuriated in the intoxicating mix of flavours on offer. At the end of the starters, Rod declared he couldn't eat another thing, but, remarkably, he changed his mind when the main courses arrived.

For these, Nga Luong had prepared lemongrass chicken, soy-stewed pork and eggs, and shaking beef. There were two kinds of rice and even more sauces. All accompanied, of course, by whisky and Belgian beer. Rod drank less of the latter than before. He was building up his fitness for the imminent start of the rugby season. He was, incidentally, still living at Vicky and Bob Root's, though now officially classed more as a lodger than a foster child.

Throughout the evening, the conversation flowed. Though Rod had been tentative at first, he was soon talking as much as the other two. What they all shared was a love of knowledge. Whatever subject was raised, at least one of them knew a bit about it and the others wanted to know a bit about it. Their conversation ranged from why cats don't like swimming, via the ingredients of the recipe for Coca-Cola, to how medieval stonemasons built cathedrals.

At the end of the meal, Major Bricket said, 'You know, I think we ought to do more of this.'

'Eating lovely meals?' asked Rod.

'No. Solving murders. We are a good team. Each bringing different skills to the table ... on which table, of course, we will continue to have those lovely meals. What do you say? Shall we work together? And look out for more murders to solve?'

Nga beamed. 'I like the idea.'

Rod beamed even more broadly. 'So do I!'

'Good,' said Major Bricket. 'Right, now, Nga, I think we need a fortune cookie.'

'Oh, that's just a stupid thing I do for tourists. I—'

'I think we need a fortune cookie,' the Major repeated. 'To give us luck on our journey to becoming a team of investigators.'

'Very well,' said Nga Luong. She thought for a moment, then pronounced, 'If you wear sandals, the sand you shake out of your shoe will soon be replaced by more sand.'

'Brilliant!' said the Major. 'Henceforth, let that be our motto!'

'But,' asked a bewildered Rod, 'what does it mean?'

'It means whatever you want it to mean,' said Nga Luong.

'And therein lies its beauty,' said the Major.

They all laughed. Then he said, 'Do you know what's been really odd about this case?'

The other two shook their heads.

'The butler did it,' said Major Bricket.